WHEN STRONG WOMEN AWAKE

STEVE BANKO

NFB
Buffalo, New York

NFB
NFB Publishing/Amelia Press
119 Dorchester Road
Buffalo, New York 14213

For more information visit Nfbpublishing.com

For Lynn and Devyn, two of the strongest women I know

PROLOGUE

"When strong women awake, mountains will move."
Chinese proverb

MY OLD BOSS WAS LOOKING at me with a waggish grin I'd rarely seen on that weathered face in all the time I'd worked for him.

"I've missed you, *vriend*," he said, still insisting on using his native Dutch for "friend." "I've had no one to argue my political views with since you've been gone."

Truth be told, I'd missed him as well. When I worked for him here in Cabo San Jose, down Mexico way, we used to close his bar, La Hacienda, and we would argue, cajole, and insult each other's political theories over several Dos Equis'.

"Well, you might be able to expound those theories with your new friend there at your feet," I said, "if only you weren't standing on his ear."

Finn's foot was firmly planted on the side of the thug's head. I thought I saw a little blood leaking from the bad guy's ear.

"This piece of garbage? What would this *bendejo* understand about politics? He's lower than worm shit, the worse kind of scum."

My buddy, Finn Bakker, had invited me down to Mexico a week ago to help him sort out a little problem that involved the teenaged daughter of one of his waitresses and a group of assholes who thought trapping young girls into a life of sex would be a good line of work. Finn had helped me out several months ago during my futile attempt to run away from some problems that befell me back in Buffalo NY.

While my career as bartender/bouncer/waiter/confidante was short lived, it did give me time to regain some perspective and to make a new friend, or *vriend*, as Finn would say. So when he called and asked for my help, I couldn't refuse. I'm glad I didn't. The guys who were abusing these young girls were exactly as Finn described: lower than worm shit. The ringleader was a wanna-be gangster who thought no one would care about a few poor young girls gone missing. He surrounded himself with a bunch of what Finn called "lover boys." These lotharios would wine and dine and romance young girls. When the hook of young love was sunk deep enough, the boys would tempt the girls with a runaway marriage or a future some place far from the poverty of Mexico. If the girls fell for it, they would wind up as captives. If they didn't, the faux romeos would move on to another unwitting girl. The standard promise was to take the girlfriends to the States where a golden future awaited the "happy" couple. This particular band of no-goods made the mistake of running afoul of Bakker. He was former Dutch Army who had seen his share of what makes a soldier a proud vet. His business gave him entre to all kinds of people, including a few who directed him to a few others who knew a guy who owed the guy a favor … you get the picture. The girls were being held in an old garage in nearby Cabo San Lucas. Finn figured they wanted them there to service the tourist trade that vacationed in the resort city. I was a little taken aback when he said our initial rescue plan would be a two-man operation.

"The same advantage that gave us intel," he said, "works the other way too. The more people who know what we're up to the more likely our plan won't be a secret."

That made sense. An informant is an informant and information can flow in any direction. But when we found out where the girls were, some of Finn's more trusted employees asked for help in the rescue. He wisely avoided using any of the relatives of the girls to be retrieved. Some lumps and bruises were one thing. A murder would be something else. There was no point in testing the patience of the cops. Dope dealing was something they could and did often turn their collective backs on. Human trafficking offended even their situational morality.

The plan was pretty simple. I would be the horny gringo looking to buy the favors of some young women. Once they opened the doors to let me in and show me the goods, Bakker and a couple of guys would burst in and start kicking ass. The remaining allies would go around to the rear entrance of the building to make sure no one escaped that way.

I knocked heavily on the garage door.

"*Hola chicos*," I yelled, "I'm looking for some *putas* and have *mucho dinero!*"

A slide in the door opened and took a gander at me. Satisfied I wasn't the *policia*, the big garage door groaned open. Three guys were inside, and one had a pistol stuck in his waistband.

"Amigos, I need some girls for a big party tonight," I said, pulling a wad of cash from my pocket. The booze I'd splashed on myself before knocking made me smell like a drunk.

"Why do you come here?" the guy with the gun said. "Who told you to come here for putas?"

"The taxi driver, *conductor de taxi*," I said, laughing. I could see the other two guys start to flank me. They probably just wanted to roll me and throw me out.

"We got no girls here, gringo. *Pierdase* – get lost."

With that, the guy on my right grabbed my shoulder. One of the first things I ever learned about fighting was never fuck around with preliminaries. If you can't avoid a fight, get right to it. This guy just wasted his intention by touching me without trying to disable me. I took a half step toward the punk and jammed my elbow under his chin. The crunch I heard told me I'd either broken or dislocated his jaw. Next, I had to disarm the dude with the gun. I kicked him square in the nuts and he went down on both knees. The guy on my left was stunned by the sudden violence of my attack and hesitated just long enough for me to spin around with my right elbow and catch him one to the temple. Then I slammed my knee into the nose of the guy with the gun. That knocked him backwards with his ass on his heels. I yanked the gun out of his pants, hit the eject button to get rid of its magazine and slid the action back to eject the round that was in the chamber. Finn and his buddies burst into the garage just in time to see the bullet bounce off the concrete floor. The Dutchman pulled the gun bearer off the floor by his hair.

"I will ask but once, *el cabron* – where are the girls?"

The guy pointed to a storage container in the corner of the garage. Bakker rendered his thanks by punching the guy in the nose. We found them huddled in a corner of the container, using each other for comfort. When the girls were loaded into the back of a truck, Bakker shook my hand.

"I knew I could count on you, and I am glad I did," he said.

"You should always know I've got your back, vriend, and you can count on me whenever you need me."

Bakker reached into his pocket and pulled out an impressive wad of American greenbacks. I waved him off.

"Finn, this was on me," I said. "I wouldn't dream of taking your money."

"Well," he smiled, "that's the first time I heard you say that. The last time I saw you, you were selling clothes to buy a plane ticket back to the States. Now you don't want my money? You have more wardrobe to sell off?"

Bakker didn't know about the big score my friend Lexi and I had made in Buffalo at the Central Terminal a few months prior to getting his phone call and I saw no point in telling him about it.

"I'm good, Finn," I said, "and I still have some duds to wear."

"Do you want to stay a few days at the Hacienda?" he asked, "or are you in a hurry to get back up to that place named after an animal that never lived there?" Finn still labored under the mistaken notion that my hometown was named after the animal called "buffalo," more accurately known as the "bison." There is a semi-true and less than semi-interesting story about how Buffalo NY got its name, but I didn't want to get into all that with Finn.

"I appreciate the offer, Finn, but I'm heading home, where I don't have to worry about assholes kidnapping young girls. I have some things to take care of back there."

"Don't be so sure about that, Coe. The money involved in this demented enterprise makes it hard to resist even in Buffalo. Keep your eyes open to the possibilities.

"This 'thing' you have to take care of – what's her name?"

I smiled back my response. He didn't know it, but Bakker was right. I had to get back to check in with the woman who occupied permanent residence in my brain but often left that space in constant disarray.

"Come, Coe, I'll drive you back to the airport."

CHAPTER ONE

W ITH ANOTHER BRIEF ADVENTURE concluded, my mind reverted to the subject omnipresent in my head - Lexi Crane. We've had a complicated relationship ever since she arrested me back when I worked for the Mayor in Buffalo City Hall. I thought we rekindled an old flame when we worked together to solve the mystery of a long-forgotten robbery and recovered a ton of cash stemming from that robbery. I might have thought making that kind of score should carry some romantic weight. But it didn't, at least not yet. Right after we cashed in, Lexi announced that she was heading off to Turks and Caicos on vacation, I thought I heard her say "we" instead of "she" until she informed me that she was going with her old partner from the Buffalo Police Department. On the plus side of a very negative situation, the old partner was a woman. But I still thought Lexi and I had something special after we found the money. In her defense though, that unfortunate incident in the mayor's office did ruin her career as a cop. She actually could have been the commissioner at some point so maybe she had grounds for still being pissed off. So I sipped my Corona and sulked about my muddled relationship. The two hours spent in the Dallas-Ft. Worth air-port didn't clear much up for me nor did the three beers I drank waiting for my flight. But the beers let me catch a catnap on the trip to Buffalo. I got off the plane stiff and sore and tired, so I decided to catch a workout at KC Fitness. I'm still not sure if that was a good idea or not. It started out good with me pounding the heavy bag with all the frustration welling out of me. It ended differently though when I noticed the object of my romantic daydreams saunter into the gym. Her trip to the Caribbean made her even more beautiful to behold. Her skin was always flawless but now it was flawless and bronze. Her black hair now had streaks of something that I swore were rays of the sun. I wasn't the only one who was dazzled by her looks, but I was the only one who was equal parts happy and pissed off to see her. I walked over as casually as I could.

"What the hell?" I said, a little too loud and with a little too much anger in my tone.

She looked at me with a coy smile dripping with more pity than anything else.

"Nice to see you too, Coe," she said. "Miss me?"

I wanted to throw her down on a mat and kiss the hell out of her, but I knew she would probably kick my ass. Lexi was once one of the best female athletes in New York State. Colleges all over the country offered her free rides for any of three sports she excelled at. Then there were the other schools that sought her for her academic prowess. But her dad was shot to death when some punks held up his liquor store and Lexi gave up the chance at collegiate excellence to become a cop. We met when we both showed up at a community meeting, her representing the police department and I representing the mayor. I took one look at her and was smitten. We became an item, and I spent the best days of my life with her; that is, until she had to arrest me. But that's another story.

"When were you going to tell me you got back?" I said.

"Whenever you answered your phone," she said. She had a point. I'm not a big cell phone guy. I didn't even take it to Mexico.

"Oh yeah, the phone … well tell me now - when did you get back? … How was the trip? … Did you have fun?" I was hoping she might just say it was okay because I really didn't want to hear she was killing it in Turks.

"Coe, it was glorious. I really needed that trip. You have to go some time."

"I thought I might be invited to go this time."

"I needed some time with my bestie," she said. "It's been a while since Cat and I spent any time together. Her job has been rough on her and I knew she needed a break."

Cat was Cat Redmond, actually Catherine, but 'Cat' ever since she got on the police force. Buffalo has a penchant for nicknames, whether you want one or not.

The knowledge that she was there with her best friend might have put some of my jealous fears to rest but looking at Lexi all tanned and golden and drop dead gorgeous had my mind racing as to what might have constituted glorious.

She noticed me staring. Helen Keller could have noticed me staring. She wasn't a fan of my looking at her so she reverted to form and gave me a punch on the shoulder. She was as fond of doing that as I was of hating it.

"Stop staring! By the way, where the hell were you? And why didn't you answer when I called?"

"I had a little junket myself," I said with a smile, "and you know I always forget my cell phone."

"Well, I thought you might been longing to hear my voice after two weeks and remembered it this time." She was smiling and I loved that smile. "So where did you go?"

I filled her in on the general details of the trip without getting too specific.

"You and that Dutchman didn't break any laws, did you?"

"We may have bent a few but it was for a good cause." When I filled her in on the cause she leaned in and kissed my cheek.

"That is a good cause. I'm glad you didn't go down there for fun."

"So you can go off for two weeks in the sun but when I go somewhere fun is off the table?"

"You learn fast, champ." Then she gave me the second punch of the day. "I need to get to work. Give me in an hour and you can buy me dinner."

She sauntered off to meet with her Muay Thai instructor while I switched over to the speed bag. I needn't have bothered. I was way more interested in watching Lexi than keeping my eye on the bag. I turned her on to Muay Thai before we ventured out on our exploits in and around Buffalo's Central Terminal. I'd been exposed to it prior to my semi-successful southwest Asian experience with a government agency but Lexi took to it like a duck to water. Already a terrific athlete and already a skilled martial arts fighter, Lexi combined speed and power as though she'd written the manual on the stuff. I focused on my bag for a few minutes until I heard the pop of her leg against the heavy bag. I could generate some power with my kicks, but Lexi made me feel like a newbie. The sound of her shin punishing the bag made everyone in the gym stop to see her spin and bounce and jab and whip her leg around like a scythe cutting through weeds. Of course, I'd seen her in action when the two of us took on a bunch of gangbangers at the terminal. I almost got a broken nose while admiring her cutting down the bangers with those long leg whips and her slashing elbows instead of focusing on my target.

Kevin Cunningham, the owner and a friend, watched alongside me.

"She is something," he said. "Such grace and balance … she's a natural."

"She's been a natural at everything she's tried," I said. "She could have taken college rides in any of three sports. She was a phenom on the police force. Mayor Culhane had her pegged as a future commissioner."

"No kidding?" Kevin said. "What happened?"

"I happened," I said and before he could ask any more questions I went over to the weights and started some dumbbell curls. Kevin didn't take the hint and followed me over.

"Something tells me there is a great story behind your last comment." With that, he punched me on the arm and walked off.

"You have no idea," I said to his back.

Thirty minutes later, I was sweaty and tired and sore – the good kind of sore you get when you push yourself and your body responds to the challenge. I headed to the locker room to wash off the fatigue and await the object of my affection. She was about half an hour behind me, which is pretty good for Lexi. She came out of the locker room with damp hair still sun streaked and glistening and smelling of soap.

"So where are you taking me, big boy?" she said.

"You pick. We're close to Cole's and Pano's and not too far from the Bijou."

"I'm hungry," she said. "Let's go see Bea."

Bea is the proprietor of a fine little spot downtown and one of our great friends. The Bijou boasts some terrific food and Bea's warm welcomes are just about as good.

"My car or yours?" I asked.

"My, my, my," she said. "You've come a long way since you came back home six months ago. You didn't even have a winter coat when you came back. We can take your yuppie-mobile. I know you want to impress me."

Her comment was an understatement. I had barely enough money to get from Cabo to Buffalo when I got her call about a cockamamie quest to look for what amounted to a buried treasure. Now, after solving the mystery of the Terminal and with a little help from a mother I didn't know I had, I was pretty flush. And my yuppie-mobile was a nice year-old Audi A6. Despite her own new-found fortune, Lexi held on to her Jeep Wrangler. As we drove the couple of miles to the Bijou, I wasn't so sure this dinner was a good idea. Lexi started out tame enough, talking about the sun and the beaches and the food in Turks. But she got way too enthusiastic in her description of her triumph in the dance contest at a joint called the Blu Bar. "Dance contest" conjured up all kinds of images of locals and fellow travelers dancing with my … well, I'm not sure what she is and I'm not sure I can even call her mine, but you understand, right?

We walked into the Bijou, Lexi with her two week-long sun-kissed body and me with my seventy-two-hour incandescent light bulb "tan" and were greeted with a hug and kiss from Bea.

"Where have you two been? Lexi, you look gorgeous. Coe … well, you look like Coe."

Ah, Bea … such a kidder.

For ten minutes, Lexi regaled our friend with details of her vacation. I was hoping that she embellished some of those details to make me jealous, but I couldn't be sure which details.

"Coe, you didn't go to the Caribbean with this beautiful lady?" Bea said.

"I couldn't go, Bea. I had some business to attend to in Mexico."

"Business? What business was more important than keeping an eye on this beauty? You must be insane."

Insane with jealousy, I thought. I didn't have the gumption to tell Bea I wasn't invited.

Whenever we venture into the Bijou, it is futile to order. Bea always makes us something special and by special, I mean indescribably delicious. Today was no exception. She brought out enough veal Osso Buco to feed an infantry platoon for me. Shrimp Fra Diavolo for Lexi. Bea left us to try to eat the feast she set down but not before kissing me on the top of the head and giving me some advice.

"Enough of this business stuff. Start paying attention to this lady."

I wanted to tell her to give Lexi the same advice about me but thought better of it. We waded into our meals with appropriate gusto before pausing to let things settle.

"Tell me about his business that brought you back to Cabo," Lexi said. "Human trafficking?"

"Yeah, some gangster wannabes were trapping these young girls into relationships by promising them marriage and life in America. But they were planning on selling these kids to older banditos. I guess there's a lot of it going on down there."

"That's disgusting," she said. "I take back what I said about not breaking laws. I hoped you kicked some serious ass."

Then we ate until the button on my pants begged me to stop. Bea bagged up the copious leftovers and we went back to my car. As I drove back to the gym to get Lexi's car, I made a note to myself: when harboring licentious intentions toward your whatever-Lexi-was, remember not to overeat. Instead of horny, I was sleepy. Just my luck, I thought. She's going to want to play, and I am not going to be able. I shouldn't have worried. As we neared KC's, Lexi said she wanted to sleep in her own bed.

"I'm beat, Coe. Just drop me off, OK? We can get reacquainted later, all right?"

I put on my sad face; secretly thankful I didn't have to sweat performance anxiety tonight.

"If you say so," I said, as we pulled up behind her jeep. She leaned over and gave me a big wet kiss – the one I'd been waiting for since I saw her. This woman knew all my buttons and took great delight in pushing them.

I don't know why I thought of it at that moment, but I stopped her before she got out of the car.

"Hey, Finn said something to me before I left Cabo. He told me to keep my eyes open about the kidnapping and prostituting of young girls here. Have you ever heard of it around here? Finn says it's a big-ticket crime all over the world."

"I haven't had any experience with it, but I'll check with my contacts at BPD tomorrow and let you know."

"And don't forget about getting reacquainted."

"How could I?" she said with a wink. Another button pushed.

CHAPTER TWO

THE NEXT MORNING I felt almost as stuffed as I did at the Bijou. I threw on my running clothes and shoes and did a hard run from my condo building up Delaware Avenue into Forest Lawn Cemetery. I found peace in the quiet of the obelisks, statuary, and gravestones. On this morning, a wisp of fog was just starting to burn off. On a good day, I might see some deer meandering through the headstones looking to graze. On a great day, I can spot the albino doe foraging among the markers. Forest Lawn is more than a cemetery. Not three miles from the heart of the city, it's one hundred and sixty acres of serenity. I powered passed Mirror Lake and around the Field of Valor where Buffalo's veterans are interred. I was really working up a sweat as I exited through the majestic arch that stands as a silent sentinel at the entrance. I crossed Delaware Avenue and headed north into the Olmsted Park of the same name and did an easy lap round Hoyt Lake before heading back to West Ferry. The park is part of the legacy of Fredrick Law Olmsted who came to Buffalo just after creating New York City's Central Park.

I now lived in a two-bedroom condo at this gorgeous building that was built in 1929. The exterior was done in something called Gothic Revival. The entrance was something to behold. It was sold to me as Venetian Gothic Revival. I didn't care what the style was. To me, it was simply beautiful. And it had gargoyles! No shit, real gargoyles. How cool is that? Truth be told, though, I live here because my mother lives here. We don't live to-gether and her unit is three times the size of mine but we met here and she confessed to being my mom here. She also filled in a lot of the blanks about the Central Terminal caper Lexi and I had completed. Before the Terminal thing, I was living in a shack in Cabo San Jose. Now I lived at one of the best addresses in Buffalo. Like I said, cool, huh?

I took a shower and decided to take a ride out to South Buffalo to see my father's war buddy, Eddie Murray. "Murman," as my old man called him, lived over a spiffy Irish bar he owned called Shaughnessy's. I took city streets to time my arrival before Eddie got busy with the lunch crowd. My timing was perfect. That happened a lot except when I was dealing with Lexi. When I pulled into the parking lot Ed was standing in the doorway admiring the covered patio he just had installed. It gave the place about fifty percent more capacity and on a gorgeous day like this the place would fill up from the outside in. During my travels I'd encounter the usual side-eye glances from people when I told them I was from Buffalo. The jokes would begin immediately about snow. I told such folks life in Buffalo was like being pregnant every year: we waited nine months for the three beau-tiful summer months. Once, while in Cabo, a woman from Alabama made some snide remark about snow. I reminded her of where she called home.

"Sweetheart, when the snow melts my house is still there. Can you say that about the tornados that rip through Dixie every spring?"

She had no response.

"Hey, Mur, the addition looks great," I said.

"Hell yeah it does," he said. "I owe you for this, kid."

In a different world, he might have owed me, since I financed the con-struction. But Ed and my father helped Lexi and I during our terminal caper and I like to pay such favors back. The episode didn't exactly make me independently wealthy, but it did make me independent.

"Pal, that was the least I could do to repay you and my dad for helping us out."

Truth be told, what I gave Eddie was way out of proportion to compen-sate for the little favor they did us but I'm good like that.

"Have you called the old man lately?" he said, patting me on the back as we went inside.

"No, I haven't. I just got back from Mexico and haven't had much of a chance."

"Mexico? What the hell were you doing down there? I thought you closed that chapter."

"I did, Ed, but my old boss needed a hand with something and I couldn't refuse."

We went inside and sat at the bar. Eddie's bartender Alyssa brought over two Buds.

When she went back to fill some waitress orders, I told Eddie the whole story.

"You keep fucking around down there, you're going to get hurt," Murray said.

"What was I going to say when Bakker asked for my help? The guy was good to me when I was down and almost out."

That's kind of an understatement. I went south after the problem I had while I worked for a former Buffalo mayor. The incident cost me my job and I could live with that. But it also ended Lexi's career as a Buffalo cop and I couldn't stick around after that. I was playing baseball in Mexico for beer money when Finn saw me hanging around his bar. We had some interesting conversations so he decided to keep me around on his payroll. I didn't make a lot of money but I did make a good friend.

"So these assholes actually sell girls?" Murman said after hearing my tale.

"I guess it's more prevalent than we think," I said. "The cops down there have better shit to do than chase down missing teenagers and there is a lot of cash to be made."

Then I told him about what Bakker had said as I left.

"Here?" Mur said. "No fucking way. Nobody could get away with that shit around here."

"I hope you're right," I said. "These scumbags are the worst. These girls we rescued had bruises all over them and they were terrified. Finn told me there was a ton of money to be made selling and working girls. And we both know money is the universal language." We drank quietly for a few minutes then the place started filling up. That was my signal to let Eddie get back to work. He walked me to the door.

I drove off feeling good that my dad and I had a friend like Ed. But I couldn't get the image of those frightened girls captive in that storage container out of my mind. Who does shit like this, I wondered, and could this kind of thing really happen here?

I decided to make another stop.

My half-sister Sheila is one of the honchos at the Historical Society. She is also gorgeous. I didn't find out we were related until my impure thoughts about her reached a level that should have necessitated confession. Thank goodness I was so into Lexi. Sheila and I share a mother who is also stunning. Go figure, huh? She was a huge help in Lexi and I finding our way with the terminal business. Sheila is every bit as smart as she is beautiful and every bit as conniving as she is smart. In short, Sheila's quite a gal.

I walked in to the Historical Society building and said hello to Vera, the guardian at the gate. She crinkled up her nose like she smelled limburger cheese. She's crazy about me but is a master of disguise.

"Hello beautiful," I said, facetiously. "Is Sheila in?"

Vera just sneered and pointed to a staircase with her nose. Vera's not big on conversation. I went down the stairs and saw Sheila at her desk. She looked as good as ever, although she would probably look good coming out of wind tunnel. She gave me that big smile and rose to meet me.

"Hello Coe, my bro," she laughed.

"Feeling poetic today?" I said and we hugged.

"Where have you been? Mother said she hadn't seen you in the building for a few days."

We sat in facing chairs and I told her of my most recent exploits. When I finished, a strange look crossed her face.

"Does Mother know?"

"No," I said. "I didn't think it prudent to tell her where I was headed and certainly not why."

"I wish you were that prudent about not going down there, Coe. Mexico is a pretty nasty place and getting involved in that dirty business is dangerous."

Then she rose and gave me a kiss on the cheek.

"That's for being chivalrous." Then she smacked me in the back of the head.

"That's for taking too many risks."

I still wasn't used to the women in my life hitting me.

I told her how I kept revisiting the image of the girls in the dark of the stage container.

"My friend told me that this kind of stuff is prevalent all over the world because of the money involved," I said. "Do you think this stuff could be going on here?

"The craving for money makes anything possible," she said. "That is not to say I've heard of anything like that in our fair city. But could it be possible? We used to be a terminus for the Underground Railroad getting people out of harm's way. Who's to say that the reverse couldn't be true as well?"

"That's what I'm afraid of. As long as I've lived here I've never heard anything about this kind of thing."

"So you need my help, correct?"

"Only insofar as passing along any information or rumors or innuendos you might pick up in your travels around town."

"You must have a low opinion of the circles I travel in, Coe," she said, but she was smiling.

"You know what I mean. Just let me know if you pick up any noise about anything like this crap with young girls. Please?"

"Of course I will. Am I to assume that I am not supposed to tell Mother where you've been?"

I stood up and gave her a kiss on the forehead.

"I'll tell her … not just yet though."

"Don't wait too long, Coe." Sheila had her serious face on. "She cares a lot about you and you wouldn't want to mess that up."

"I promise," I said, bounding up the stairs two at a time.

Next stop, Cole's.

CHAPTER THREE

Donnie Joe must have seen me walk by the window as he already had a cold Budweiser on the bar. DJ was almost as legendary as Cole's itself. The place had been a Buffalo fixture for more than half a century and still numbered regulars in the hundreds. It was a prime spot for collegians from nearby Buffalo State College and the other surrounding schools as well as older guys who just loved the place. Donny Joe had a huge following of his own including me.

"Where the hell have you been?" he said.

Buffalo's like that. Don't show up for a few days and people start to wonder. Don't show up for a few weeks and people wonder when the wake will be.

I gave him a cock-and-bull story about wrapping up my affairs in Mexico and the conversation quickly passed on to baseball. I was a decent ballplayer in college and was a hundred or so batting average points away from being pro but I did get paid for playing for the Chihuahua Dorados a year ago. We shot the shit in between DJ taking care of other customers and I had another beer. I was about to take a slug out of the bottle when I got a whack on the back that almost made me swallow the bottle.

"Jeez-us Christ!" I said, wheeling around, expecting to flatten someone's nose only to find my other old boss, Shamus Culhane. My beer was dribbling down my chin as I tried to say hello. I needn't have bothered. Shamus gave me one of those big bear hugs he was famous for.

"How you doing, Jericho?"

Culhane is the only guy who can get away with calling me that. It is my given name but it is not "my" name. "My" name is Coe. It seems my old man, Vietnam War hero Joshua Jeremiah Duffy, got his handle from my Bible loving grandma. The old man went by Josh but when it came time to name his only son he made my name a paean to his mother by reaching into the Old Testament and pulling out Jericho. At least that's what my old man told me. But calling me Jericho when I was growing up would get the offender an ass-whipping. I made sure everyone knew my name was Coe.

"I'm doing okay, Shamus. If it were any better it would be illegal. How about you? What's going on with you?"

"Just loving life," he smiled. "Retirement is better than I imagined."

We toasted that and the beer started sliding down my throat; a sure sign I should stop. Shamus eased into our conversation seamlessly and it seemed like old times. Mercifully, my phone rang. Lexi was calling me. I moved away from the bar to answer.

"Hey, how are you doing?"

"How are things at Cole's?" she asked.

"What makes you think I'm at Cole's?"

"For one thing, I can see you through the window." I looked up to see her waving at me. "For another, you aren't with me so where else would you be?"

She had a point.

"Why don't you come in and have a beer?" I said. "Shamus is here."

"I can see that, dumb ass. I'm looking through the window, remember?"

She had been such a kidder. But I knew she wouldn't want to mingle with Shamus. She was still smarting from arresting me in the mayor's office even though it was more than a year ago. She had been on light duty after recovering from being beaten by two street punks and was at her post in the reception area of the office. I had a bit of a confrontation with a half-drunk job seeker in front of her desk. The episode ended with the drunk minus a tooth and getting his nose broken. Lexi had no choice but to arrest me as this all took place a few feet from her. Rather than testify against me at trial, she quit the police department and left town for a few weeks. That was the end of my career in public service and our budding relationship.

It occurred to me that I shouldn't be standing inside with Lexi standing outside so I hung up and headed for the door.

"I'll be right back," I said, over my shoulder.

Lexi kissed me on the cheek.

"I checked with Brett Joseph about this trafficking stuff," she said. "He said they had been making a few more prostitution busts than usual but nothing more than that."

"So nothing out of the ordinary?"

"He didn't say so but I think he's holding something back."

"Why do you say that?"

"Just a feeling – a cop feeling."

I decided to change the subject.

"What are you doing for dinner?" I said. "Want to come by my place and we can order something or do you want to go somewhere?"

"What I want to do right now is go workout. I'm still stuffed from the Bijou food orgy. I'll come by your place after the gym. Now get back inside and play nice with the other boys – and don't you dare get drunk. I'll see you around seven."

With that she went to the jeep and sped off as I went back inside. Mindful of her last command and of Sheila's insistence on seeing our mother, I finished my beer, said my goodbyes, and headed home.

Back in my own digs, I splashed some water on my face, swished my mouth with Listerine, and took the elevator up to my mother's suite. "Sweet" would have been a more apt description. My mother, who I didn't know was my mother until we'd finished with the Central Terminal adventure, was once a consort of the head of the local mob. But that was after she'd fallen for my brilliant but damaged old man. She knew about me well before I knew about her and she came through big time when Lexi and I needed a boost. I knocked on the door.

"Come in, Coe." Ah, Sheila. She must have told her mother of our conversation and her suggestion that it was time to say hello to mom.

I entered and took in the sights. My mother lived on the top floor of our building and had spectacular views of the city. But my mother, one Marsha McCartan, was pretty spectacular herself. The years, and her accumulated wealth, had been good to her and she still warranted stares any time she entered a room.

"The wandering traveler returns," she said, smiling.

"Marsha, I was gone three days; four counting travel. I hardly count that as wandering." This late in life it was hard for me to refer to her as "mom."

She kissed my cheek and ushered me over to her Wexler sofa. The Plinth marble coffee table was set with a silver service from which she poured coffee for us both.

"As you can probably tell," she said, "Sheila has filled me in on what took you back to Cabo."

"I figured as much," said. "But I couldn't say no to someone who did so much for me when I was down and almost out. Besides, it was for a good cause."

"Perhaps," she said, "but you must have figured out by now that the people engaging in that filthy business are the worst kind of scum."

"Of course I have, Marsha. That's one of the reasons my brief foray into that world was so satisfying."

She sipped her coffee and was silent for a minute or so.

"Coe, you know I love you dearly."

"Of course I do and I return that love."

"If that is true, and I have no reason to doubt you, please promise me you will have nothing more to do with this disgusting business."

That surprised the hell out of me.

"Why would you say that? I would think you would want me saving as many women as I can."

"For one thing, they aren't all women. The scum that indulges in this kind of modern slavery has little concern for gender. Men, women, boys, girls … this filth looks at them all as a commodity; something to be exploited, traded, and thrown away. Think about how amoral and ruthless and utterly depraved they are to engage in this business. They have no regard for human life. All they care about is money and they will do anything they can to keep making it. They wouldn't hesitate to eliminate any obstacles to profit and I don't want you to be one of those obstacles."

To say I was stunned would be a gross understatement. I knew of my mother's history before I knew she was my mother. She had lived a life of luxury as a gangster's woman but she had stood up to anyone and everyone who tried to turn her into something she was not. She'd raised her daughter the same way but hearing Marsha now made me think about the look I saw in Sheila's eyes back at the Historical Society. That was the look of fear, a look I don't recall ever seeing in her before.

"Marsha, before I left Cabo, my Dutch friend told me not to discount the possibility of that kind of thing happening here. Do you know anything about that?"

"No, I don't, Coe, but I'm not sure I would tell you if I did. I really don't want you delving into that kind of cesspool."

We passed the next fifteen minutes or so with small talk about what else we were up to. Unlike me, my mother had a full social life in and around the city and she caught me up on all the latest local news. The conversation slackened and I took my leave, promising Marsha I wouldn't do anything stupid.

But I had my fingers crossed behind my back. I have made a life of doing stupid stuff.

Lexi showed up at my place still damp from the shower and smelling like lavender. She didn't come empty-handed. She brought a six-pack. Apparently, my drinking was allowed if I was in her company but I didn't complain. Instead, I filled her in on my new found family's reaction to my interest in human trafficking.

"Wow," she said. "From the little I know about Marsha I wouldn't think there would be very much to cause that kind of reaction."

"That's what I'm thinking but I only know a little more about her than you do. Think I should ask my old man if he can shed some light?"

"What can it hurt? If he knows, he might not tell you but that's where you are now, correct? But let me go back to something you said earlier. How interested are you in this trafficking shit? And if your ex-mobster mom is scared, should we be?"

"First of all, my mom isn't an ex-mobster, Lexi. She hung around with some mobbed-up guys but that doesn't make her a mobster. Secondly, I am more interested in what the subject arouses in people than the subject itself. What makes it so scary? Do your cop friends react this way? I don't get it."

We pondered the subject for a little while but couldn't arrive at any sound conclusions. I was still lost in thought when Lexi put down her beer, took my face in her hands, and kissed me like I hadn't been kissed since we got sort of rich with the terminal thing. She was trying hard to win our tongue-wrestling match and I was all too happy to let her. She stopped and looked into my eyes.

"I missed you," she said, and round two of the match began. And here I thought she might have gone to the Caribbean to get away from me. Or maybe she had. At this point, I didn't care. I pulled gently on her hair to get better position for my kiss. I must have done okay for when I broke it off, she let out a giant sigh. That was the end of the beer and the beginning of something much better. I lifted her off the couch and carried her into the bedroom. I laid her down and kissed down her neck and over to her throat and down again, unbuttoning as I went. I got into her cleavage and she squeezed my face between her breasts. If I could pick a way to die, it would probably be suffocating between her tits. I kissed and licked and she reached around behind her back and undid her bra. Her breasts were a stark white against the deep tan on the rest of her. I kept kissing down her stomach.

Well, I thought, she wasn't sunbathing nude. Then I stopped thinking with my big head. When I came up for air, she was smiling.

"Coe Duffy, you are a marvel."

CHAPTER FOUR

When I woke up she was long gone. Lexi was like that. She had this thing about waking up in her own bed. After we reacquainted ourselves a couple of times, I slipped off to sleep. I was vaguely aware of her leaving the bed but was too spent to say anything. I also knew there would be no dissuading her from leaving. After taking in as much of her lingering scent on my pillows as I could, I headed to the kitchen. I called my father down in Ft. Myers while making my coffee. I needed to understand why everyone was so damned scared to even discuss this trafficking business. Josh Duffy had been in love with my mom after he came home from Vietnam with a couple of Purple Hearts and worse, a purple mind bruised and battered by what he'd done and seen. Seagram's VO was his medication of choice and he self-medicated often. It's funny how the damaged mind can rationalize things. As deeply in love with Marsha McCartan as he had been, he separated himself from her love to spare her the ordeal of tortured anguish he was dealing with. But not before he planted the seed that would become me. Of course, I wasn't privy to any of this until Lexi and I embarked on our adventure seven months ago. After Marsha and my dad split, she wound up as the "companion" of the capo of the Buffalo mob. I guess she had a thing for bad boys, which made me even more curious about her reaction to our conversation about traffickers. I figure she'd already seen or heard or knew about the exploits of gangsters so what was one more crime.

My father's answering machine picked up on the fourth ring. I left him a message and put on my running togs. I was out the door and running south on Delaware Avenue toward downtown. The morning air was still cool and the sky was that brilliant blue that made me feel energetic. Ten minutes later I was running around Niagara Square, which is really a circle. It's dominated by a nearly hundred-foot obelisk that was erected as a memorial to President William McKinley who was assassinated in Buffalo in 1901. It's also government central with City Hall, city court, federal court, the FBI and some other buildings around the ring. I once occupied an office in City Hall as chief of staff to the mayor. It wasn't all that long ago I was in that building but so much had passed since then it seemed like light years ago. I headed back up Delaware, pushing hard against the steady grade that would keep rising for a mile or so. I sprinted the last five blocks to my building and was a sweaty mess when I reached my door. I checked the answering machine but my father hadn't called. Naturally, he called while I was in the shower. I got him on the line while I was still toweling off and explained why I was calling. My normally voluble dad was quiet. I knew that wasn't good.

"What has you poking into this shit?" he said, finally.

I told him of the mission that took me back to San Jose del Cabo but he cut me off before I could finish.

"Are you fucking crazy?" he shouted. "Those whacked out *banditos* will cut your balls off and feed the rest of you to the sharks."

I had suddenly, and unconsciously, touched the third rail in the Duffy clan.

I waited for a full two minutes while my father ranted before cutting him off

"Take a breath!" I yelled into the phone. I must have surprised him because he did. "I raise the subject with my half-sister and she blanches. I tell my mother where I've been and she sounds more scared than I've ever heard her. I tell you about it and you hit the fucking ceiling.

"You want to tell me what's going on or do I keep digging and find out on my own? You should know by now that the best way to get me to do something is to tell me I can't.'

I could hear him breathing so I knew he was still on the line. When he did speak, there was something in his voice I'd never heard before.

"What I am going to tell you is for your ears only. Do you understand? You must never repeat a word of it to anyone under any circumstances. Any word of what I am going to tell you ever gets out and people could die."

I was floored.

"People like who?" I said.

"People like your mother."

The story he then told me explained a lot and just about knocked me off my feet.

•••

My mother, Marsha, found out she was pregnant with me before she started her dalliance with the mobster. I was only eight weeks old when she contacted my old man. She told him you care for your son or I put him up for adoption. My father still drinking himself to death but the news that he had a son snapped him out of the morass of self-pity and guilt that was eating at him. He told Marsha he would raise the child but she made him swear that he would really be a father to the boy and stop the self-destruction. My dad gave her that pledge and turned himself around and became a real father.

"Eddie Murray played a big role too," my father said. "He had a sister who never married and she was your nanny."

"What does any of this have to do with mom?" I said.

"Just shut up and listen!" he snapped.

Not long after giving me to my father, Marsha found herself hanging around the mobster. My father theorized that she had seen this guy in her future before giving me to him but that's not germane. One night, Tony takes my mother on one of collection runs, picking up money from various businesses. They get to a strip club where the real money is made by the strippers turning tricks. Tony made my mother wait in the car while he transacted his business inside. My mother is sitting in the car that's parked near the back door of the place when the door opens and a big thug shoves a scared girl on to the asphalt. My mother doesn't know what's going on but after the goon goes back inside my mother leaves the car to go to the girl who looked to be a teenager. She helps her up and sees the bruises on her faces and arms. She also sees the slight swelling in the girl's tummy. My mom was no saint and knew much of what her boyfriend was doing but this way was too much. She gave the girl a handful of money and wrote an address on a piece of paper. She told the girl to get a cab to that address and someone there would help her. Then she got back in the car to wait for Tony.

"What was on the piece of paper?" I asked.

"The address of a convent," my dad said. "She had an aunt who was a nun. She called her Sister Mary Mea Culpa because she went around all day apologizing to God for 'sins' she never committed. Marsha knew if the girl went to see Mea Culpa she'd get help."

I pieced the rest together.

"So the pregnant teen goes to the convent and mom's aunt helps her out. I still don't get why she was so mad at me about going to Mexico."

"You have some of the story, kid," my father said, "but you are missing the important part." Then he filled in the blanks.

The nuns took in a lot of young women in the same situation as the teen sent by my mom. They had a section of the convent where they housed the girls, fed them, and had doctors look after them. My mother's aunt called her a couple of days after the girl arrived at the convent.

"Where did you find this poor girl?" she asked and my mother gave her the details.

"Mea culpa, mea culpa, mea maxima culpa," the nun said. "The doctor said he'd never seen a case like this. This girl had been pregnant before and either she or someone else aborted the child. The abortion damaged her beyond what our doctor had encountered before."

The nun went on, telling my mother that the teenager was now being weaned off whatever drug she's been on but the prognosis for the fetus wasn't very good. She also told my mother that the girl had a couple of badly healed fractures that might never have been treated by a doctor. As her aunt went on about the terrible condition of the girl, my mother was getting more and more incensed by the minute, wondering where the girl had come from and how she'd gotten caught up in this shitty life. She ended the call telling her aunt her she'd cover whatever treatment the girl needed and to keep her informed as to her condition. Her next call was to my dad. She wanted him to find out about this girl in particular and the girls in the strip club in general.

"I had a lot of connections at the police department," my father said, "and I was able to get a little background on what was going on. That's how I learned some of the trafficking end of this.

"It seems the strippers slash hookers were all from the U.S. My cop buddy said a couple of girls had broken away from the bar and sought help from the cops. They both told similar stories. One was a pretty good soccer player in school and a guy approached her family claiming to run an elite camp for athletes like their daughter. He insisted his camp could give her the special skill that would make her good enough to get a scholarship to college."

"And the parents never checked this guy out?" I asked.

"Some parents are gullible. Some want to believe their kids are so good this was all possible and others are plain stupid.

"Anyway, the guy tells the parents he will waive the fee for the camp, which was a couple grand. The parents are convinced their daughter is a special case and are giddy she's going to get this elite training.

"The girl goes off with the guy and never saw another soccer ball again. The asshole beat her and raped her before he sold her off to some other assholes who brought her to Buffalo to whore for them. The other girl was living on the street."

Dad went on to say that Marsha wanted to know what the mob involvement in the process was and he told her what the cops had told him.

"The police said they couldn't be sure about mob involvement in getting the girls. They could only trace that part to the club owners. The mob only wanted their rake from the profits of the club. Your mother pressed me on that part. She wanted to know if the guys were part of buying and selling these girls but my sources didn't think they were."

"Damn," I said, "I guess I know why she's so angry about this shit."

"No, you don't," my father said. "Not yet, anyway."

"What the hell … there's more?" I said.

There was a lot more and my father continued the story. When he was done, I was speechless.

The girl my mother rescued gave birth to a somewhat healthy girl. The baby was small and needed a lot of post-natal care but she survived. The mother was not so lucky. For reasons known only to her, the girl snuck out of the convent and made her way back to the strip club. The next time she was seen, she had been beaten to death and stuffed in a dumpster a couple blocks away. But it was the coda to the story that was the stunner.

"So what happened to the baby?" I said.

"Eddie Murray had a spinster sister so we put our heads together …"

"We?"

"Yeah, we – Murman, me and Marsha – and of course Mur's sister. She took the baby and raised her till she was five or so. Me and Marsha paid her and she did a great job. By then, Marsha had had enough of Tony Calvane- so and his crew and she took the child."

"Wait! Marsha raised the girl and the girl is now Sheila?"

"That's not the best part," my father said. "One night Marsha heads over to the strip club and waits outside until closing. She sees this Mario some- thing, the owner of the joint, heading out to his Porsche. She speeds into the parking lot and hits the guy going about fifty. The asshole goes flying over the hood and slams into the windshield. Marsha slams on the brakes and the dick goes sliding off. Then she backs up and runs over the guy to make sure he's dead."

"She told you this?"

"She didn't have to. I was there. Me and Eddie."

I knew my father and his sidekick, the Murman, had been involved in some serious shit before. I knew they had taken "extreme" measures to deal with a debt collector sent by their bookie. I knew they had been live-on-the-edge guys. But now my mother was a murderer too? What the fuck?

"Okay," I said, "she murders the guy ... then what?"

"We prefer to think of it as 'killing' the guy," my father said. "This prick deserved to die."

We're talking about killing a guy and my father is arguing definitions. I was expecting Rod Serling to show up any minute and tell me I was in the Twilight Zone.

"How did you get rid of the body? What did you do with the car? Jesus, there are so many loose ends to this."

I needn't have worried, he said, they had it all figured out.

"Marsha got in my car while Murray took the damaged car to an abandoned railroad line a few miles away and torched it," he said. "Then we picked him up and took Marsha home."

He told this story like he was telling me what he had for dinner that night.

"Jesus, Dad, does Sheila know this? Six months ago. I didn't know Marsha was my mom, I thought Sheila was my half-sister, and tonight I find out mommy's a murderer too?"

"Grow up, asshole," he said. "I just told you what these scumbags are doing to young girls. You were in Afghanistan. You know the world is full of bastards who deserve to die and I'm pretty damned sure you whacked some of them yourself so don't go all Sister Mea Culpa on me.

"You asked me why your mother is upset at your new interest and I told you. Your mother is one of the best people I know and more than that, she's one of the best people you know so get off your goddamned high horse and take the story for what it is – a fucking morality tale where good triumphs over evil! And Sheila doesn't know and she better not ever find out."

A morality tale, I thought. Toto, we aren't in Kansas anymore.

CHAPTER FIVE

I WAS STILL TRYING TO process all that I'd just heard. I sat for a long time with visions of my murderous mom dancing around in my head. I hadn't known of her existence six months ago. Since then, I'd discovered in rapid order that she was once my father's girlfriend, then consort to the head of the local mob, then a fabulously wealthy woman, then my mother. Along the way, I'd discovered a half-sister who was instrumental to Lexi and I solving a mystery and getting a bit of wealth. Now, I learned that my mother was simultaneously a savior and executioner.

And I thought my life was messed up after Lexi had to arrest me. Christ, that now seemed like the best of times. So I did what I always did when mental acuity didn't match the mental challenges – I ran. The cemetery was still my favorite spot. The peace and serenity of the place was a contradiction to the morass churning in my head. There aren't many places where you can find an Indian chief, an American president, and super freak artist Rick James all together. But they are all resting at Forest Lawn. I like running through the roads along the Field of Valor that looks like a miniature Arlington Cemetery. It's a sad, proud sight on Veterans Day and Memorial Day with the little flags snapping in the wind. Forest Lawn has seven Medal of Honor recipients among its "residents." Only Arlington has more. Today, I went through the main gate off Delaware Avenue and went hard up the main road, past Mirror Lake and across Scajacquada Creek and curled around to make it over to the veterans' plots near Main Street. By the time I headed out of the cemetery, I was drenched in sweat despite the spring chill. I took it easy back to West Ferry, wishing I could lose the muddle in my head as easily as I'd lost the sweat. After I showered, I sat back on my new Joss and Main "Feliciano" sofa Marsha had picked out. My life was spinning like a dreidel when all I really wanted was for it to normalize for a while. I didn't know what to do with all that I had learned but I knew there were precious few people with whom I could share it. All of the usual suspects were out: Marsha, my dad and Murray were all co-conspirators. Sheila was out of the question. I guessed I could tell Lexi and might in the future but there was no real point in dragging her into this right now. I am not a very religious guy. Going to war makes you question a lot about whatever your religion of choice taught you about the inherent goodness of man and abject prohibition about taking human life. But I have encountered some people who I recognize as not just true believers in their faith but legitimate practitioners of it. My father introduced me to one such guy a while ago. The guy was a Franciscan friar but before he'd worn the robe, he wore a uniform like my dad and like my dad, was a grunt in the moral quicksand that was the Vietnam War. This guy, a man named Ryan Mc-Caffery, processed the physical and moral pain differently than my father and most vets had. He committed himself to a life of living his faith and helping others along the same path. Father McCaffrey was a one-man operation in a small, impoverished parish in a troubled part of Buffalo. I reasoned that with all the other challenges facing him, my own issues might not seem extraordinary. I also thought that my extravagant donation to his parish might also curry some favor.

I called him and he answered on the first ring.

"Well as I live and breathe," he said, "How are you Coe?"

"Hello Father. I'm OK, I think. But I'm hoping you might spare a few minutes to help me sort through some stuff."

"Stuff is my specialty, Coe. Want to come to St. Pat's or shall we talk on the phone?"

"I'd rather talk to you face-to-face, Father, if that's OK."

"Of course it is. Why don't you buy me dinner at Chef's, and we can come back to the rectory and talk?"

I smiled to myself at the facility the friar had in sliding into a free meal.

"Can we do it tonight?" I asked.

"Yes, I'm rather hungry."

We made plans to eat early and go back to the rectory for the meet.

Chef's is and has been a staple in the Buffalo restaurant scene for longer than I've been alive. It's sort of the outer marker of the downtown area and not far from the hockey arena and the baseball stadium, making it a great location before or after a game. It still had red and white checked tablecloths and a tradition of great Italian food. My only reservation about it was the portions made me want to lie down after eating there. But now, I was energized by what I wanted to bounce off Father McCaffrey. His rectory wasn't but five minutes from the restaurant.

We settled into some worn easy chairs and sipped some brandy the friar had handy.

"What's on your mind, Coe, and how can I help?"

"The first part will be easy, Father, telling you what's on my mind. I'm not sure there is an answer to the second part." With that, I spent the next thirty minutes relating the story my father had told me a few hours ago. We sat in silence for a few minutes before McCaffrey spoke. When he did, I wasn't sure he heard or understood what I'd just told him.

"Coe, are you familiar with the movie 'Shrek'?" he asked.

What the fuck, I thought, I just told the priest I'm the spawn of murderers and he's talking about an animated movie? He must have read my frustration because he didn't wait for my response.

"There is a point in the movie where Shrek tells the donkey that ogres are like onions – they have layers. The ogre is telling the donkey not to make judgments on the mere appearance or reputation of ogres; that beneath their rough exteriors there are other facets of ogres not readily apparent."

"So my father is like Shrek?" I said, with a little frustration seeping through.

"Pretty much ... yeah," he said. "There are quite a few layers to your father, and I think you are only just beginning to peel back some of them. I met your father in the white heat of combat; he was not only trying to keep himself alive but keeping his men alive. I saw that kind of responsibility destroy weaker men but it made your father stronger and harder. He accepted the role as a leader and a teacher and was one of the finest soldiers I ever encountered. He was fearless in taking on the Army bureaucracy as he was facing the enemy. But to be a good soldier you have to be a bit ruthless. That quality doesn't easily translate to being a good and decent man."

I had seen my share of lunatics, leaders, and losers during my own war time experiences so I was getting what McCaffrey was saying.

He continued.

"I think that's why your father had such a hard time adjusting to life after war. He needed to find another layer. You were that layer. Once you were born and in his life, he found the humanity that had been so elusive for him. In caring for you, he was also caring for himself."

"Okay," I said, "but once he found his humanity, he still regressed to being a thug?"

"I think you are mischaracterizing him," the friar said. "He was never a thug. But he was hard and he was ruthless and he was vicious and violent. Above all, he was a survivor. When he was threatened, he responded."

"Are you really trying to defend him?"

"No. I am trying to explain him as I know him. And if I were you, I wouldn't be so quick to condemn him nor the methods he employed to protect your mother. Your father is loyal to a fault, and he loved your mother almost as much as he loved you."

"What about you, padre?" I asked. "Are you Shrek in brown robes? Do you have layers?"

"Hell yeah," he said, laughing. "I was the one who taught your father to be a combat soldier. What do you think that makes me? I found my purpose in this kind of service the same way Josh found his in fatherhood. And if you are lucky, you will have a few layers of your own to keep peeling back."

I was almost finished with my brandy when I asked him what I was supposed to do with my newfound knowledge?

"Wise men temper their knowledge with wisdom," he said.

My quizzical look indicated I had nary a clue about what he'd just said.

"Look, knowledge is knowing that a tomato is a fruit," he said. "Wisdom is knowing not to include it in a fruit salad."

With that, he drained his glass and stood. I did the same and offered him my hand. He blew passed it and hugged me.

"Never forget that the two people you are doubting are two people who love you more than anything in the world," he said.

"I won't, Father, and remember I'm always good for a dinner or two when you get hungry."

***

I'd just about made it into downtown when Lexi called.

"Where are you?" she asked. She's prone to avoid small talk.

"On my way home. Where are you?"

"I'm at home – yours, not mine."

"You are in my apartment? How did you get in?"

"Your doorman has a thing for me." That wasn't surprising. If I had a doorwoman chances are 13 to 5 she'd have a thing for Lexi. "Bring home something for dinner."

"I already had dinner at Chef's," I said.

"Well, just get something for me then. You can watch me eat."

Every once in a while, I needed a reminder of why I was so smitten with this woman. This exchange was one such moment.

"I'll stop at Cole's …"

"You will like hell! I don't want common bar food."

Ah Lexi, let me count the ways.

"Well, what do you …" Have I mentioned I don't often finish my sentences when talking to her?

"I already called Hutch's and told them you would be picking up the yellow fin tuna."

This girl thinks of everything.

"Whose name is the order under?"

"Yours," she said. "It makes it easier for you to pay that way."

I could imagine her smile when giving me the instructions. She likes being the boss. She hung up before I could say anything else. If I hadn't already eaten, Hutch's would have been a great choice for both of us, not just Lexi. It wasn't all that much out of the way and the order was ready when I got there so I had them throw in a couple pieces of apple pie. I had to eat something while she was enjoying her dinner.

When I got to my elevator, Simon the doorman, started to tell me about my visitor. I gave him a smile and a wave.

"I already spoke to her, Simon. Thanks." If he thought he needed to apologize for letting Lexi up, he didn't show it. Note to self: don't have attractive female guests with him on duty. There's no telling what his libido might mean for my security. When I walked in the door to my place, Lexi was busy arranging plates on the dining room table. I put her dinner on the table and pulled out the deserts. She looked pleased.

"I'm surprised you didn't order the dessert," I said.

She winked at me.

"I didn't want to be presumptuous." See why I love her?

While she arrayed her food on her plate, I opened some wine.

"Pinot Noir okay," I said.

With her mouth full of fish, she only nodded her assent while I poured. She paused her meal long enough to sip the wine.

"This is delicious," she said. "What kind is it?"

To answer, I had to check the label. My mom and my "sister" picked out the wines for my table.

"Bernardus Pinot from California," I told her, glad she was impressed.

"Tell Sheila she has good taste." So she wasn't that impressed, with me at least.

We were starting the pie when Lexi revealed the reason for her visit.

"Tell me again what started you on this human trafficking kick?"

I reminded her of my brief foray into the muck when I went down to help my old boss.

"And that's it? You thought the word of some bar owner was worth your time?"

"He's more than some bar owner," I said. "He's a friend who has his ear to the ground and knows stuff."

Lexi laughed and ate some more pie.

"Well, he certainly does know stuff," she said. "You remember Lindsay Zgoda, my friend from the police department?"

"The chick with muscles in her hair? Hell yeah I remember her. I would see her working out and be amazed at how strong she was. She still on the force?"

"Yep, but that's only the beginning of my story. Lindsay has a sister, Abigail, who's a flight attendant and I was talking to her about your interest in the trafficking thing. I had to convince her I wasn't busting her balls but when I did, she told me about something her sister encountered on a flight a month or so ago."

I pushed my pie aside to devote my full attention to Lexi telling Lindsay's story.

"The flight was from Houston to LaGuardia," Lexi said, "and Abigail takes note of a young girl traveling with this old dude. Abby figures it's the guy's daughter or niece or something harmless like that but as the time passes she notices the guy never lets go of the girl's wrist. She thinks that's a little off but figures that the girl might be afraid of flying. But as Abby passes through the cabin she gets the feeling something is off about this situation so she tries to ask the girl if she needs anything. When she does, the guy does all the talking. The girl sits by mute."

As Lexi goes on, I'm wondering if these traffickers could be so brazen as to use schedule airlines. But as the story unwinds, I guess they are that brazen.

"By now," Lexi says, "Lindsay's sister is beyond suspicious so when the guy orders a beer, Abby brings the girl a water and before she gives it to the girl she gives her a glimpse of the napkin and some writing on it. Abby puts the water down and watches the girl from several rows away. The girl holds the napkin away from the guy and reads it by the reflection in the window. Then she shoots Abby a look like a deer in the headlights and now Abby knows something is wrong. She goes back to the guy and the girl and starts clearing the glass from the girl's table and deliberately spills some in the girl's lap. Then she takes the girl's hand from the guy and says she'll bring her to the rest room to clean some of the mess up. The guy tries to resist but Abigail won't take no for an answer and she gets the girl back to the john in the back of the plane."

By now, I can see all this unfolding and I gain a new respect for these flight attendants.

Lexi can see I'm invested in her tale now and she gets a little melodramatic.

"So this fearless flight attendant hustles the girl to the back while the dude is trying to look behind him to see where the girl is headed. Abby doesn't talk to the girl until she opens the bathroom door and completely blocks the view of the guy. Then she asks the girl who the guy is. With broken English the girl tells Abigail she doesn't know the guy and he's taking her somewhere."

Lexi is almost breathless as she wraps the story up with the flight attendant returning the girl to her seat and alerting the pilot to the scheme. When the plane lands in New York, no one gets off the plane until after the air marshals get on and take the girl and the guy into custody. When the feds started questioning the guy, he stonewalls for a bit but breaks down when they are getting ready to move him to federal detention.

"The guy admits to bringing the girl to New York to turn her over to another guy who was supposed to bring her to … ready for this? …to Buffalo so she could be brought to Canada."

I could tell Lexi was jacked on the information. I was jacked because I was right. But neither of us should have been jacked knowing we might be hunting modern slavers. I wondered why we hadn't learned of all this way before now. And why had it taken a guy in Mexico to alert us to the development?

CHAPTER SIX

LEXI MUST HAVE REALLY liked dinner and the wine. I surmised as such because she spent a long time thanking me. When she was done, she thanked me again and again. She was like that, allowing her actions to take the place of a lot of words. Damn, how I loved her action. I fell asleep with a big smile on my face and her warm body tucked in nicely next to mine. But when I woke from my reverie, she was gone as per usual, and I was left with the afterglow of her gratitude and the nagging thoughts of the story she told me of the hero flight attendant and the young girl she saved. I was still trying to wrap my head around the story my father told me and now I get to process the reality that Buffalo could be a hub of trafficked people. What the hell?

I skipped a run, showered, dressed and called my old boss and buddy Culhane. He was the former mayor but he still had his finger on the pulse of what was happening in our fair city. He agreed to meet me at Pano's for breakfast after insisting it was my turn to pay. We sat in the window and watched the traffic roll by on Elmwood Avenue while the server poured coffee and took our order. I decided to jump right into the reason I'd brought Shamus out.

"Hey Boss, have you heard anything about human trafficking hereabouts?"

Shamus bent over his coffee and leaned in closer to me.

"What have you heard?" He was a happy-go-lucky guy by nature but now he had a worried look on his face – a look I hadn't seen much of during our time together.

"I haven't heard much," I said, "but what I've heard I don't like."

Then I proceeded to tell him about Mexico and Abigail the hero in flight. Shamus sat in silence until our server dropped off breakfast.

"This is getting bad faster than I thought," he said. My look must have told him I had no idea what was getting bad.

"Some of my contacts in the PD have been sounding a semi-silent alarm about an uptick in reports about missing girls. The girls are young and good looking and come from good families. They found one of the girls two weeks ago down near the Pennsylvania border. She was face down in a little stream and had been beaten to death."

Culhane went on to explain that the Buffalo cops and the sheriffs down south started comparing notes and it turns out the girl had been seen a lot at one of the casinos down there. She's been kicked out a few times when security figured she's been hustling tricks The post-mortem tox screen revealed the beating wasn't the cause of death.

"She'd actually been killed with a hot shot of heroin. The poor kid had track marks between her fingers, between her toes ... everywhere but her arms."

"That's a little different than the scenario down in Mexico," I said, "but the same crime. You co-opt the kids and keep them hanging around with juice. You turn the kids into slaves and when they are used up you throw them out like garbage."

"That's the play," Shamus said, "and that's the angle the cops are looking at."

"But these girls are local, right?" I said. "They aren't being flown in here from points south."

"My guys say the issue they're dealing with is more runaways and throwaways: kids who take off or get kicked out of their homes. They wind up on the street and some dude finds them and treats them nice for a week or two before they drop the hammer. Then it's too late. They're dependent in ways they could never have imagined and they are turning tricks to get high."

Now I knew why my mother and father hated the abusers so much.

Shamus and I parted on Elmwood Avenue. He headed to his consulting business downtown and I took a slow walk back to my place. Elmwood Ave is one of those eclectic streets you find in college towns like Higuera Street in San Luis Obispo or Second Street in Austin. It's lined with little shops and stores and more than a few bars and restaurants. Buffalo State College is to the north and downtown Buffalo to the south. Summer was coming on and the near-empty branches of the trees along the street were punctuated with green buds. The street looked great three seasons of the year but best in late spring when the leaves started to pop. I was about halfway back to my place when a young woman approached me with her phone extended toward me.

"Hey dude, you seen this girl?" she said.

I looked at her phone and saw the face of what could have been most young women in Buffalo. The face was framed with blonde hair, neat and clean. She had sad eyes and a mouth that looked like it wanted to smile but couldn't. The girl in front of me was another story. She had piercings in her eyebrow and nose, and three in one ear. Her hair was scraggly and streaked with purple. I figured the total number of piercings to be north of nine, but who was I to judge?

"I don't think so," I said. "What's happened to her?"

"We think her boyfriend grabbed her. He's in the Army and he wants to get married before he goes off to fight in some shithole or another, but she don't want to so we think he came home here and is taking her some place to do something she don't want to do."

The girl looked frantic and that made me want to help.

"Is the guy home on leave?" I said.

"I don't know about stuff like that," she said.

"Well, we could find out and that might make your search a little easier."

"How do I find out?" she said.

"You probably couldn't but we might."

"Who's we?" she said.

I looked around to see if there was any other possible combination of people that might form a 'we.' There wasn't.

"You and I. We might be able to find out. We would do it easier with me helping because I might have some contacts with the military that could provide some answers."

"You would do that, man?"

"Sure. If she's in trouble, I would like to help."

"Sweet. How does this work?"

"Give me his name and a phone number where I can reach you. I'm on my way home and when I get there I can call in a favor or two and I can get some context about the boyfriend."

"Some what?"

"Some background … some idea what the guy is up to."

"Okay. That's good."

With that she grabbed my hand and whipped out a Sharpie. She scribbled on my hand.

"Promise you'll call me, right?"

"Yep, as soon as I know something I'll let you know."

Without a word, she headed down the street and thrust her phone at a woman walking toward her and started her spiel. I wondered if every woman I encountered in my life would be abrupt.

I got back to my place and spun through my fat Rolodex to find the number of a friend with whom I shared some tough times in Afghanistan. He went to work in the Department of Defense and just happened to owe me a favor. Saving a guy's life does accrue some benefits.

Elmo "Moe" Maloney came on the line with a familiar "what the fuck do you want?"

"Hey buddy, great to talk to you too. How are the wife and kids?"

Moe had been engaged twice without result and was very sensitive to that fact. It's always nice to know where to stick the needle. When we dispensed with the pleasantries and got down to the reason for the call, Moe told me to hang on the line while he got the information on one PFC Ronald Norton.

"Your soldier is AWOL from Ft. Knox Kentucky … been absent without leave for six days," Moe said. "His CO said the guy presented himself as highly motivated and has no blemishes on his record."

I told Moe why I was checking on the guy and where the MPs might locate him.

"Thanks, old friend," he said, "don't call so frequently in the future."

He hung up before I could sneak in the last word.

So the poor, love struck private had decided it might be worth a possible court martial to try to talk, cajole, or coerce the object of his affection into marriage. Poor bastard.

I kept my promise and called the number on my hand The voice that answered was far different from the on I'd encountered on the street.

"Yeah."

"Hey, I got this number from a young woman a little while ago. She was looking for a friend who went missing. I told her I would try to help. I have some information about the guy she thinks might have abducted her friend."

"Dude, I don't know shit about shit like that"

"Well, the girl does, DUDE, so just tell her I called and if she wants to know what I found out she can call me back." Then I ended the call. I decided I didn't like being called "dude."

I went to the refrigerator to get some water when the intercom buzzed. When I answered it, I was pleasantly surprised to hear Lexi's voice.

"Hey, Coe, are you decent?" Like I would tell her if I wasn't.

"Yep, come on up."

I heard her knock and had half a mind to strip down and answer the door buck-assed naked. I was so glad I resisted. When I opened the door, Lexi was there with her friend Cat Redmond.

"Hey, come on in." I held up my hand to give a wave to Cat and instantly regretted it. The scrawled phone number was still in my palm. Lexi noticed too. She gave me a serious punch in the arm.

"What the hell is that?" she said, "some chippie's phone number you collected?"

I dodged another blow to my arm and told her the story of the girl on the street.

"My chivalrous Coe, defender of the downtrodden," she said. "You are forgiven."

Forgiven for what, I wondered, but didn't have the guts to ask.

"So you found out this guy is absent without leave and might be up to no good," Lexi said. "What's our next move?"

I was puzzled.

"'Our' and 'move' have me a little befuddled," I said. "I did what I said I would do but I see no point in doing anything further. It's up to the military police now."

I could see this answer was not what Lexi expected.

"Come on, Coe. You've been poking around all this trafficking stuff. Why don't we pitch in for this missing person gig?"

"First of all, you aren't a cop anymore and I never was. So while the sound of a ten eighty-three or whatever number a missing person is might tickle your fancy, I don't know what else you or I could do."

"Maybe I can help," Cat said. She pulled out her cell phone and punched in a few numbers.

"Hey Darlene, It's Cat. Can you check and see if we have anything on a missing person: white female, early twenties, blonde hair? Sure ... nothing too urgent call me when you can."

"See," Lexi said, "that was our next move. Now we see what the BPD can tell us and go from there."

I tried not to look skeptical but I must not have carried it off because I got another whack on the arm.

"Show some enthusiasm, partner."

I showed the women into the living room and Lexi took over from there, showing Detective Redmond the rest of the place all the while sounding like an ersatz real estate agent.

I took a seat on the couch while the tour was being conducted. When the two came back to the living room Cat seemed impressed.

"This is some great place, Coe," she said. "Very nice indeed."

Lexi piped in before I could say thank you.

"His mother found the place and picked out most of the furniture," she said.

I was about to mention the great view from my balcony when Lexi jumped in again.

"Coe, show Cat the view from your terrace."

I took Cat over to the French doors that opened on to the terrace.

"On a clear day, you can see the mist from Niagara Falls," I said, and pointed off to the north. "If the terrace went all the way around, you would see the east side of the city all the way to the Central Terminal and beyond."

I still recall the view from my mother's terrace that included the terminal and her belief there was always a dark cloud associated with it.

"This is beautiful," Cat said. "It must have cost an arm and a leg."

"Just an arm," I said. "The leg went for the furnishings."

That got an evil glance from Lexi. She hates it when I'm funny.

I offered the gals a drink but they declined and said they were heading out to do some shopping. Before they left, Lexi gave me a bigger than expected kiss and whispered in my ear.

'I love showing you off." She winked and said she'd call about dinner later and just that quickly, I was alone again.

CHAPTER SEVEN

I WAS WATCHING NICOLE WALLACE on MSNBC when the phone rang. When I answered, the voice was familiar, but it wasn't who I expected.

"Hey, this is Dora, the girl from this morning. My friend told me you called."

"I wasn't sure I would hear from you again. Your friend didn't seem very interested in what I was telling him."

"Yeah, he can be like that. What did you find out?"

"Well, Ronald Norton is indeed AWOL from his Army base. That means he's absent without leave and ..."

"I know what AWOL means, asshole, but did you find out where he is?"

Gone was the imploring gal from this morning and replaced by this pain in the ass.

"Asshole? Are you kidding me? I went to the trouble of asking his status and now I'm an asshole? You are on your own, sweetie. Good luck."

"No ... wait, dude, I'm sorry. I'm just worried about my friend. What should we do now?"

"Well, first of all, my name isn't 'dude.' It's Coe. What you should do now is get in touch with the Army and tell them what you know about his intentions toward your friend. They might send some MPs to try to find and arrest him. At the very least, they will know where to start looking for him."

"Can't you do that? You told me you had connections."

"I told you I had contacts and I contacted a friend who gave me the information about PFC Norton. So that's it for me. The rest is up to you."

"Well, fuck you very much, Coe, and thanks for nothing."

I stared at the now silent phone and thought that's what I get for trying to help someone. The world is overstocked with assholes and ingrates these days.

I went out on my terrace and tracked the westward movement of the sun as it slid slowly toward the silvery waters of Lake Erie. It didn't take long for the vision to calm me down. Let the assholes fend for themselves, I thought, and relaxed in the reverie of coming sunset. I was dozing off when Lexi called.

"Hello beautiful," I said.

"Hmm … thanks, I needed that. I'm beat. Cat walked my ass off today."

"Oh God no!" I shouted. "Not that beautiful ass!"

That actually got a chuckle out of her. Making Lexi laugh is one of the best things I can do.

"I assume you're calling about dinner," I said.

"Yeah … about that …"

I sensed a night alone coming up.

"I was going to suggest an elegant *al fresco* dinner tonight," I said.

"Coe, I'm really tired out and I don't feel like getting all dolled up, even for you."

"That works for me. I was thinking about a lovely tube steak fully dressed and washed down with Aunt Rosie's Loganberry."

"Tube steak? …"

"Yes, dear. I want to take you to Connors' on the lakeshore for a hot dog or two."

"Hmmm, are they open for the season already?"

"Yep and I'm sure I can get Karen to reserve a prime table for us. And along the way, we can catch glimpses of the sunset."

"You sold me, you smooth talker. I'll pick you up in ten minutes but I have to warn you, I might be a bit ripe from all the walking Cat and I did today."

"Your ripe beats any other woman in an evening gown and Chanel Number 5."

"Right answer, you stud. Someone sounds horny."

"You mean 'hornier', right? I'm always turned on by the sound of your voice."

"Damn, Coe, if I wasn't so damned hungry I might just wrestle you into bed. See you soon."

I threw on a clean St. Bonaventure t-shirt and pocketed my cash while I splashed on some cologne. The only dark side of this scenario was Lexi driving. She was a good driver but she had that Jeep that drove, well, like a jeep. I like the smooth ride of my Audi. But it was a small price to pay for a night with Lexi. I headed downstairs knowing she would want me waiting for her instead of the other way around.

Simon went around to open the passenger side door for me. I jumped into the seat and Lexi leaned over the give me an unexpectedly wet kiss. I assumed that was for Simon's consumption as she smiled at him as we drove off.

We headed south to the tall Skyway bridge that afforded a panoramic vista of the expanse of Lake Erie. We drove past the skeleton of the old Bethlehem Steel plant in Lackawanna. It was once one of the largest steel mills in the U.S. but all that remained now was the rusting hulks of the few buildings not cannibalized for scrap. We traveled along the former Hamburg Turnpike, skirting the edge of the lake and went along the old route to the lakeside. It was tree-lined and smelling of new buds and it always gave me a sense that all was right with the world, even when I knew better. Neither of us talked very much but Lexi's hand played with the hair on the back of my neck, making the trip even more relaxing. The parking lot for Connors' was remarkably empty. In a few weeks, once the summer season kicked off, the lot would be constantly packed. The char-grilled hot dogs were worth the 30-minute drive. I was pleasantly surprised to see Karen Connors Erickson behind the counter. Her family had operated the stand for more than seventy-five years and she knew most of her customers by name.

"Coe Duffy, what a nice surprise. What brings you out here this early in the season?" she said. She came around from behind the counter and gave me a hug.

"And who might this vision be?" she asked.

"Karen, this is Lexi Crane. Lexi, Karen."

"Great to meet you, Lexi, in honor of your first visit to Connors' I'll make sure Coe springs for dinner."

"I like you already," Lexi said, giving Karen a hug. Me? I got a punch on the arm.

We gave Karen our order and sat at one of the picnic tables. The chill from the lake waters just across the street made Lexi snuggle a little closer for warmth. The snuggling made me appreciate the cool evening air. Our order was up and we went to the condiment table to dress them up. I am just a mustard guy – a horseradish mustard guy – while Lexi made her dog look like a veritable salad. She topped hers with enough onion to make my eyes water. She gave me a wink.

"Don't worry," she said," I've got Altoids in the jeep."

I insisted that Lexi try Aunt Rosie's Loganberry, a uniquely Buffalo beverage she said she'd never tried. It's a blend of blackberry and raspberry juices that is overwhelmingly sweet and inordinately delicious. She took a sip and smiled.

"This is incredible!" Then she smacked me on the arm again.

"What the hell?"

"That's for not making me try it sooner." Then she leaned over and kissed my cheek. I have mentioned, have I not, that I am still trying to figure this woman out.

We ate quietly, sharing way too many French fries that Karen insisted we eat. I figured I'd made a good call with Connors' when Lexi belched. She looked at me with the slightest hint of embarrassment then started laughing.

"Damn, Coe, you really know how to feed a girl."

"Glad you liked it but you need to thank the chef. I merely paid the bill."

Lexi rose and went behind the counter to give Karen a parting hug. In all the years I'd been coming to Connors' I'd never seen anyone allowed behind the counter. They hugged and Lexi promised she'd be back, with or without me.

"You are always welcome, Lexi, but when you are with this guy we have someone to pick on." Lexis gave her another hug and joined me.

"Okay, sport," she said, "now what?"

"Have you got a blanket in the jeep?"

"Yep."

I went over to the vehicle and found the blanket. It was wool and heavy and perfect for this evening. I threw it over my shoulder and pointed across the street to a place the neon sign in the parking lot identified as the South Shore Beach Club.

"The beach?" she said. "You've got to be kidding."

"Not kidding," I said, "but this blanket will definitely help." We crossed the street, leaving the jeep in Connors' lot.

We walked inside the South Shore and the place was almost deserted. I waved to Delilah, the bartender and she smiled back. The place was small and dark but after Memorial Day, people would be packed in shoulder to shoulder to taste Delilah's margueritas and listen to the music from the patio. No margueritas tonight though.

"Delilah, can we have a couple of Irish coffees?"

"Coming right up."

With the steaming drinks in hand, I guided Lexi out to the patio. The sun was dipped low in the western sky and would soon disappear beyond the horizon. But for now, it held on to the day with a blaze of burnished gold and smears of pink and white. We took two chairs and sipped the laced coffee. I tried to put the blanket around both of us but it didn't work. So I put it around Lexi's shoulders and wrapped it around her. The sky was majestic but the air was still cold.

"You are so damned chivalrous," Lexi said, 'but I've got a way we can both use the blanket."

With that, she handed me her drink, stood, and sat on my lap, snuggling close and wrapping us both in the warmth of the blanket.

"How's that my Lancelot?"

"It could only be better if we were naked."

"Now there's a thought," she said, and kissed me smelling of coffee and whiskey and onion. It was the sweetest breath I ever smelled. We sat there sipping and kissing and watching the blazing red sun fight futilely against the gathering gloom. It showed its rage in a red and gold and pink burst of color that turned the waters of the lake molten red. When night took over, I noticed Lexi's eyes start to close.

"Come on, gorgeous. Time to get you home."

She purred a little protest and took my face in her hands for another kiss. I was about to throw her on the ground and take her when she rose and smiled and took the blanket. We walked through the bar and across the parking lot to the jeep.

"You okay to drive?" I asked her.

She must have got her second wind on the stroll.

"Hell yeah, I'm okay. Let's roll."

We took the more conventional route home, driving along a four-lane road that significantly reduced our driving time but it was dark by the time we got to my place.

"You want to park this thing and come up for a while?" I asked.

She looked at me with those beautiful eyes twinkling.

"You bet!" Then she wheeled the jeep around to a visitor parking spot and grabbed a duffle from the back seat.

Yippee, I thought. She's spending the night. We spent the ride up on the elevator engrossed in a feverish tongue-wrestling match. There were no losers. She broke away for minute and took the duffel into the bathroom. I could hear her brushing her teeth. What a woman, I thought. She emerged and threw her arms around my neck and kissed me. When she broke the kiss, she smiled.

"New toothpaste," she said. "Like the taste?"

Who knew hot dogs would have such an effect on this gorgeous lass, or was it the loganberry? I didn't care. I slid her sweatshirt over her head while she wiggled out of her jeans. The sight of her in her bra and panties never got old but the sight of her out of them was even better. Lexi was still a golden tan from her Caribbean vacation. She kissed me with an intensity that was driving me crazy. She broke away from the kiss and pushed me onto the bed. She got on top of me and slid up my body to give me access to her gorgeous breast. I accepted the offer and kissed, sucked, and nibbled accompanied by the sounds of her purring and moaning. She wanted more, though, and I was so very willing to give it to her. She continued climbing up my body leaving a path of heat until she settled in over my face. She wiggled and grinded and wiggled and pumped and grabbed my hair and used my tongue to bring her to a whimpering climax. She sat there limp and mumbling to herself before sliding off me.

"Damn Coe, you are the absolute best," Lexi said, nestling into the crook in my arm.

"You ain't seen nothing yet, darling." Then I proved it.

Deliciously spent, we lay together for a long time, her nibbling along my neck and me caressing and massaging and soothing all the right spots. I was on the verge of nodding off when I was aware of her getting out of bed. I wanted to go into the bathroom and carry her back to bed but I knew it was no use. She just liked sleeping and waking up in her own bed. Before she left, Lexi kissed me a soft, lingering kiss.

"Thanks, pal. Tonight was perfect." And perfect it was ... all except for us both waking up alone in the morning.

CHAPTER EIGHT

I awoke to a couple of glorious smells: the aroma of the coffee brewing in the kitchen and Lexi's lingering scent on the sheets and pillows. It was a blessing and curse to be so enamored of such a complex woman but that sounded redundant even in the quiet of my mind.

I got out of bed and drank a little coffee before jumping in the shower. I was on my second full cup when Lexi called.

"Glad you're awake, handsome. I just got a call from Cat."

"And that would interest me why?"

"Duh, you were looking for a missing person yesterday and Cat called in to see if the cops had anything."

I'd almost forgotten about Dora the Implorer. Her rudeness just about erased her slate in terms of getting me interested in helping.

"Oh yeah ... sorry. The only thing I remember about yesterday happened last night in my bed."

"God, you are incorrigible. A couple of orgasms and you turn into an imbecile."

I hoped she was kidding.

"So what have we got?" I asked.

"A report came in on a girl with the description you gave us but it wasn't recent. It was filed two weeks ago."

"Hmm...thanks. I'll see if that info helps that little urchin out. What are you doing today?"

"I'm going to work out at Kevin's gym then I'm going to tan. I have to keep this glow you were so interested in last night."

I didn't have the nerve to tell her the part I was most interested in probably wasn't tanned at all.

"Call me later if you want to do something," I said, but she had clicked off.

With my playmate occupied, I threw on some shorts and a sweatshirt and resolved to go for a run. The sun was out but winter must like Buffalo because it refuses to let go without a fight. The temperature was creeping into the upper 40s. The air was pretty bracing when I hit the street, but by the time I'd gone a few blocks down Delaware Avenue, I was warming up, and by the time I headed through the Forest Lawn I had a good sweat going. I wound my way along the meandering roads of the cemetery until I was running by the veterans' tombstones. That made me think about the AWOL, PFC Ronald Norton. I hoped he hadn't screwed himself too badly by leaving his post even if it was to pursue his fiancé … fiancé? If he was trying to convince the gal to marry him why had she gone missing a full two weeks before he went AWOL? This wasn't adding up. My new acquaintance Dora wasn't being honest with me. So instead of shit canning her request for assistance as I'd planned, I decided to delve in a little deeper.

By the time I made it back to West Ferry I was soaked. I showered and tried to call Lexi but it went to voice mail as I expected. I left her a request for a call back and decided to call her friend Cat. That was, of course, before I realized I didn't have Cat's number. I called the Buffalo PD and asked for Detective Redmond but she was out working a case. I got dressed and headed out to see Eddie Murray. I got there before the lunch rush and he joined me for a beer. I told him the story of the missing girl, the bitchy friend, and the AWOL soldier.

"You're right," Eddie said. "This isn't adding up, unless the fiancé knows the GI is coming for her and takes off before the guy goes AWOL."

"That doesn't sound right," I said. "What if the soldier heard his fiancé went missing and then went AWOL?"

I took a long swallow of the cold Budweiser. It always tasted better after I'd had a hard run. Ed went off to check on lunch prep when my phone rang. Caller ID came up Buffalo PD. It was Cat Redmond and I asked her if she had a minute to check on the name of the missing woman. She put me on hold but was back in less than a minute.

"Coe, her name is Norton. Jennifer Norton."

"Thanks Cat, that's a huge help... "

The missing woman was already the wife of the GI, I thought. So why had the mudlark on Elmwood Avenue given me a line of crap? What was really going on here? Wheels started turning in my mind. Maybe Lexi was right. We just might need to take some next steps. The new information flipped the script that Dora had provided. So why had she lied to me? Why was she such a dick when I told her I could no longer help her? What the hell was really going on here? When Murman got back I filled him in on the new info. He didn't have an answer to any of the questions. Instead, he threw another scenario into the mix.

"Do you know how old the girl is or the GI?" he asked. I didn't know why that mattered.

"Maybe the girl is his sister," Mur said. "You need some more information about the relationship between the two. That might give you a better context for what's going on."

It's good having friends. It's better having smart friends.

"Damn, Eddie. You're on to something."

I pulled out my phone and punched in Moe Maloney's number. I caught him before he went to lunch.

"Moe, that AWOL we spoke about ... PFC Norton ..."

"Yeah, another shirker trying to beat Uncle Sam. What about him?"

"Can you get me his date of birth, his place of enlistment, anything you've got on him."

"Damn. Why did I take your call before I left for lunch? I suppose you need this info right now?"

"Only if you are going to spend all afternoon chasing some barmaid in Old Town."

"Are you shitting me? If I'm two minutes late in this office alarm bells go off. I'll text you the data in an hour."

"Thanks, buddy. You're not the best but you are on the leader board now."

He signed off in his usual fashion.

"You're still an asshole."

I thanked Eddie for weighing in and headed back north, pondering the issue of Ronald and Jennifer North and the scruffy Dora. Bouncing the problem off Eddie had paid off so I reckoned that it couldn't hurt having another source helping out so I headed to the Historical Society to check in with sister Sheila to see if she might have some insights on the issue.

My secret admirer Vera was manning her post when I came in. I blew her a kiss and headed down to Sheila's office but not before seeing Vera wrinkle up her nose like I'd just farted.

"Hello Sis. I could use some of that great intuitive intelligence of yours."

"Anything for you, Coe," she said, smiling.

I told her about meeting the Jekyll and Hyde Dora and the subsequent revelations my inquiries had gleaned.

"So that's where we are," I said, "but maybe the information I get from Maloney at the Pentagon will sort this out."

"I'm thinking Dora had some nefarious purposes in mind when she approached you. Of course, she had no idea that you would be like a bulldog with a hambone once she piqued your interest."

Sheila came from behind her desk and sat next to me. She took my hand.

"What do you intend to do with the information?"

"I have no clue," I said. "I just got my fancy tickled. I just want to see what's going on and who is zooming who. This little chick on the street seemed like she needed my help. Now I'm thinking the GI and the woman are the ones who might need me. But I'm still just gathering information."

"And Lexi, what's she doing in this regard?"

"She's kind of out of the loop so far. I haven't told her about the stuff I found out about the Nortons."

"Well, I would think that you should learn what you can and evaluate what you know then hand the issue off to the authorities. You have no official standing, you know."

"Yeah, I get it. I'll be careful." I stood and kissed her on the forehead got an intoxicating whiff of her perfume.

"That's not what I implied, Coe. I stated unequivocally that you should have no role in anything beyond intelligence gathering."

"Got it, Sis." But I winked at her. She frowned and shook her head.

I was in the car when Moe's text came in.

Norton's date of birth was 21 May 1999. He enlisted in Buffalo but his next of kin were parents who lived in Niagara Falls. That wasn't unusual. Lots of recruits had jobs in Buffalo or went to school in and around the city so they might have found a recruiter here. Indeed, Norton had spent a year at the University at Buffalo before enlisting. His specialty was classified 19K, armor crewman. He was assigned to the 10th Cavalry at Ft. Knox; nothing unusual about any of that. His AWOL status was the only truly distinguishing mark on the record. I was headed home when Lexi called. She agreed to meet me at the apartment.

She came in with her hair still wet from the shower and smelling of something floral. I shared what I knew while she drank from her water bottle.

"Something smells rotten," she said. "I'm thinking your buddy Dora is up to no good here unless she's related to the Nortons and nothing she told you would indicate that, right?"

"No, and because she seemed legit at the outset, I didn't press her on anything. When she turned on me, I figured something was wrong."

We sat on my couch and Lexi finished her water.

"Can we contact your pal Cat and she if she has anything else on the missing girl? Norton doesn't list a wife as next of kin so I'm thinking Jennifer is his sister."

Lexi pulled out her phone and was talking to her friend in seconds. Apparently, Lexi had a number for her I didn't.

"Can you check and see if there's a DOB on the missing girl, Cat? Yeah, I'll wait."

Cat must have come back on as Lexi thanked her and ended the call.

"The woman's birthday is May 21 …"

"1999," I said.

"Yeah, how did you know?"

"Same as the GI. They're twins."

That got me a punch on the arm.

"Damn, Sam! We've got something! The soldier goes AWOL because his sister is missing. Your buddy Dora is looking for the sister for something else altogether. "

"Yeah, but what? What's going on?"

"Don't worry, Coe. We're going to find out."

"And how exactly might we do that?" I said.

"The same way we solved the mystery of Central Terminal," Lexi said. "We use our heads."

Why hadn't I thought of that?

CHAPTER NINE

"First, we need to focus on what we know instead of what we don't know."

We were sitting in a booth at Shaughnessy's, we being Lexi, Cat Redmond, and I. Lexi reasoned that her detective friend might have some ideas about what to do with regard to the missing Norton twins. Once again, she was right.

Lexi said we now know Nortons are twins and that the girl I encountered on the street was full of shit. I hesitated, not wanting to jump in with something hideously obvious like we knew the GI was AWOL. Then it struck me.

"We know the parents live in Niagara Falls," I said.

"Bingo!" Cat said. "That's where you start. Find the parents. Get some background on the twins. Find out where Jennifer was last seen. Focus on what you know to find out things you don't know."

A cursory examination of the white pages revealed too many Nortons for us to cold call to find out which of them parented twins. Cat enlisted the resources of her department to find the address of record for PFC Norton, saving us a lot of time and trouble. Cat didn't come with us as she didn't have an official reason to leave her jurisdiction, so we jumped in Lexi's jeep for a twenty-minute drive to the Falls. Normal people take a bit longer to get up there but in case you hadn't noticed, "normal" is not applicable when dealing with one Lexi Crane. Her GPS took us passed the Rainbow Bridge that crossed into Canada and north toward Niagara University. We turned onto College Avenue and ended up at the corner of Deveaux Street. The Norton house was a well-kept home on a street of other well-kept houses. We went up the stairs and knocked. A matronly-looking woman opened the door and smiled.

"Can I help you?"

Lexi did our talking.

"Mrs. Norton?"

"Yes, that's me."

"Ma'am, we're helping the Department of the Army in locating your son. Have you heard from him lately?"

"Not for a week or so. He's somewhere in Kentucky learning about tanks."

"How about your daughter? Have you heard from Jennifer lately?"

With that, Mr. Norton appeared with his glasses perched at the end of his nose.

"What's with the questions?" he said. "Who are you two and why are you asking questions about our children?"

It was my turn to talk.

"Mr. Norton, may we come in and then we can explain everything?"

"Explain from right there," he said.

So I did, sort of.

I told him his son had gone absent from his base and we thought he might have contacted his family.

"We're hoping to find him before he gets in too much trouble," I said.

Mr. Norton stepped aside and motioned for us to come in. He sat in an easy chair while his wife sat on the couch next to us.

"This is not like Ronald," he said. "He's usually very conscientious and level-headed. I can't understand why he's doing this. The last time we spoke, he sounded enthusiastic about his training."

"Ronnie told us he couldn't really focus on school," Mrs. Norton said.

"That's why he quit college. He said he wanted to do something useful. That's why he joined the Army."

"What about Jennifer?" Lexi said. "Is she in school?"

"She finished a semester in nursing school and was waitressing in the evening."

"Are they close, Ron and Jennifer?" Lexi asked.

"Very much so," Mr. Norton said. "They're twins you know so they are a lot closer than most brothers and sisters."

"So if Ron thought his sister was in any sort of trouble, that might explain why he felt the need to come back here?" I said.

"It certainly would," the father said. "He'd steal one of those tanks he's driving to help his sister."

Mrs. Norton filled us in with a lot more information about Jennifer than we needed so Lexi handed her a business card.

"We want to be of assistance to Ronald and his sister," Lexi said. "If you hear from either of them, please tell them to call us at once. We want to resolve this as soon as we can so Ron doesn't face too much discipline for deserting his post."

Mr. Norton walked us to the door. Then he gripped my arm, hard.

"I don't know who you are but I was in the Army and I know how seriously they take AWOLs and I know they don't send civilians to bring them back so why don't you tell me who you are and why you are looking for my kids."

As gently as I could, I removed Mr. Norton's hand from my arm.

"Mr. Norton, we are working with the Buffalo police and we're looking into something that involves young women in the city. We are just making some preliminary inquiries into circumstances around that investigation. We are checking a lot of various leads and when your son turned up AWOL we thought we might make a few inquiries to see if that's related to what we're working on."

I gave him my card. He nodded and closed the door behind us.

"You are so full of shit your eyes are brown," Lexi said.

"My eyes are a beautiful shade of blue, in case you haven't noticed," I said. "What did you want me to say to the guy? We think your daughter is in some serious shit and your son is risking stockade time to help her?"

She punched me in the arm but she was smiling. We climbed in the jeep and headed south.

"Well, we don't know a lot more than we did before we met the Nortons," Lexi said.

"Yeah we do," I said. "We know that neither kid has been in contact with the parents so we can focus on looking around Buffalo. We sort of eliminated the Falls and that narrows the parameters."

"Parameters? Did you buy a dictionary or what?

"Hey, I'm an English major and once upon a time, words were my life."

That earned me yet another punch in the arm as Lexi sped down the highway. My phone buzzed just as we passed under the Peace Bridge.

"Hello Mother, now nice to hear from you," I said.

"Spare me the nonsense, Coe. I would like to see you as soon as possible."

"Of course. I'll be home in ten minutes."

"I'd better see you in eleven then." She hung up. This was definitely not like my mother. She was the epitome of decorum and discretion. For her to hang up on me didn't auger well for my visit. Lexi dropped me off, telling me she had to meet up with some friends. I was sort of hoping she would pick this moment to meet my mother but I was left to face the music alone – whatever that music might be.

Simon greeted me as I approached the door.

"Your mom wants to see you ASAP," he reminded me.

"Got it, Simon. I spoke to her a few minutes ago."

"Well, she called down two minutes ago and wanted to know if you'd come back yet."

Damn, I thought, she must really be jazzed but I still didn't know about what. Simon must have called up to her apartment for when I got off the elevator she was waiting at the door.

"What did I tell you about poking your nose into places it doesn't belong!"

I'd never heard her raise her voice before. I wish I knew why she was doing it now. The confused look on my face must have told her I had no idea what she was talking about.

"Don't give that dumb-assed wounded puppy look! You know where you've been poking your nose!"

That constitutes the third "first" for my mom. I never heard her swear either.

"Slow down," I said, trying to buy some time but not knowing why I needed to. "Where has my nose been that's causing yours to be so far out of joint?"

"I told you specifically to stay the hell away from that human trafficking stuff you came home from Mexico talking about."

"I have had nothing to do with any of that stuff," I said, hoping my nose wasn't growing a little.

"Then why have you been looking for Jennifer Norton?"

Damn. I knew Buffalo was a small town when it came to gossip but this got around exceptionally fast.

"I'm not looking for Jennifer, actually. I'm looking for her brother ... her twin brother Ronald. He's gone AWOL from ..."

"... Ft. Knox," my mother said. "I know about that, but what's the interest in Jennifer all about?"

She seemed a little calmer so I took her by the arm and led her to her sofa and told her the story of my chance encounter with Dora who showed me a picture of what she said was a missing girl."

"Jennifer," my mother said.

"Well yeah, Jennifer. But I didn't know that then. All I was told was that this girl was missing and her psycho boyfriend was coming to talk her into marrying him. So I told this street urchin that I would check on the boyfriend's status with the Army and now I know that the soldier was her brother, not her lover."

I filled in the details of our trip to Niagara Falls.

"And that's the whole story."

My mother rose from the sofa and walked to the east terrace. She stared out the window for a minute then turned back to me.

"Coe, that's hardly the whole story. That's hardly even the beginning of the story."

CHAPTER TEN

"WELL, WHY DON'T YOU fill me in on what you know and why you are so animated about this?" I said.

Buffalo is a small town when it comes to connections. Everybody seems to know everyone else. Hell, most people are related, much less connected. But my mother has more connections than most. Once connected to the seedier side of Buffalo life, she is now a philanthropist of major proportions so her connections extend into legitimate and not so legitimate matters. Her past isn't exactly prologue but it does give her contacts on both sides of the law. She sat back down on the couch and closed her eyes. When she opened them again, they were glassy.

"The girl is a nursing student and was waitressing at a nice place called The Shakespeare," she said. "A few weeks ago, she went out with some other waitresses on a night off. Jennifer and a couple of the older girls decided to call it a night but two of the younger girls wanted to dance and they headed off to some bar near Chippewa Street. Those two never came home. Jenny and her friends thought they might have just hooked up but when they missed their shifts at the restaurant they knew something was wrong."

She went on to explain that Jennifer and another waitress went to look for the missing girls. They skipped a shift at The Shakespeare and went to the last place their two friends had been. Apparently, asking a lot of questions in that kind of bar attracts a lot of attention – the wrong kind of attention. One of the bouncers told them that no one in the place remembered their friends and the establishment didn't want them bothering their customers. They were to leave and not come back.

"That was good enough for Jennifer's friend but Jenny must have some of your inquisitive nature," my mother said. "The other girl left but Jenny was determined to find out what happened to her co-workers. The next night, Jennifer didn't show for her shift and the girls knew something bad was going on."

"How long ago was this?" I said.

"About two weeks."

"How did the soldier get involved?"

"Jennifer had told the other waitresses about her brother and where he was stationed, so one of the girls contacted him after a couple days. He told the caller he'd be there to take care of it."

"That was about a week ago, right? Just about the time her twin went AWOL."

The tale was getting murkier by the minute; three girls missing and a highly motivated GI looking for his twin sister. This wasn't going to end well and judging from the expression on my mother's face, she knew it too.

"What are we going to do, Mother?"

"I had hoped that we might leave that to the authorities but I know you too well. What do you suggest we do?"

"I'm not sure yet but I have to do something. The GI sounds like a good kid and the sister was looking at a bright future. That's worth some effort to protect."

She smiled at me and kissed my forehead.

"Please be careful," she said, but the look in her eyes gave away her doubt that I would.

•••

I called Lexi and filled her in on what I knew.

"So what now?" she said.

"Ask your cop buddies what they know about the black hole that keeps swallowing people up. Get whatever intel you can. Call me when you can."

"What about you? Are you getting ready to do something stupid?"

"Not just yet. There will be enough time for stupid later. I just want to know a little more about what's going on."

"OK, but no stupid without me! You got it?"

"Got it." This time I hung up on her.

I called Sheila at the Historical Society. She had almost as many contacts as her mother.

"Mother told me you might call," she said. "I'm checking with some people about the place in question. I will call you when I know something that will help."

I thanked her and hung up.

It didn't take Sheila long to call back.

"Have you ever heard of a place called the Loading Dock?" she said.

I allowed that I hadn't. She told me it had been open about a month and was already attracting a lot of attention and not the kind of attention a legitimate place would want.

"Some friends at police headquarters have told me they've received some tips about bad things going on there. It might bear checking out," she said and told me where this place was.

"I would strongly suggest that you do little more than look around, Coe," she said. "The regular clientele is not regular in any sense."

"Thanks, Sheila, I already pledged my sanity to Mother so I repeat that pledge to you."

"Your fingers aren't crossed, are they?" She hung up before I could answer. I was glad she did. Me, doing something dangerous?

I thought I might need a little company to check the place out so I called Eddie Murray.

"Are you free to do a little recon later?" I said.

"Just tell me where and when and are we going in heavy or light?"

That's what I liked about Eddie. He was always up for a little fun.

"I'm thinking tomorrow night and we'll go light for the first look."

"Roger that," he said and hung up.

I fired up my MAC and checked out the area around the bar. It was a lot farther off the entertainment strip than I figured. It must have been an old warehouse in the long-abandoned warehouse district astride the rail lines that were once the commercial arteries of Buffalo. It was little wonder I'd never heard of the place given its locale.

I planned on driving when I headed south to pick Murray up. When I got to his bar, Eddie had other plans.

"Leave your ride here," he said. "We'll take this." He slid into the driver's seat of a Land Rover.

"Nice," I whistled, climbing in. I saw a big gym bag on the back seat.

"We going for a workout after the recon?" I said.

"Nope. I know you said we were going in light but I thought we should prepare for the worst while we were hoping for the best."

I opened the bag and saw a couple of aluminum baseball bats, an axe handle, and at least half a dozen saps of various sizes. While I hoped we would have no use of any of Murman's toys, I was glad we had them. It was a little after ten, we drove along Exchange Street up to a big, dark building scantly illuminated by a neon sign that simply said "Loading Dock," which is exactly what this place had been when Buffalo was the second largest railhead in the country. We timed our arrival to beat the presumed rush but there was still a line of some fifty people waiting to get in. Murray drove slowly past the entrance where a very large doorman scowled at the crowd. The building was long and low, just like the transfer station it once was. Goods came off the trains and were stored in these warehouses until trucks backed up to the dock and took the stuff to their final destinations. That's where the street took its name. Across the street, cars were parked in an unpaved space that served as a lot. We drove about a hundred yards and turned right, heading around to the back of the building. We headed along a gravel road that ran alongside the rails that were now largely dormant.

We spotted a couple of guys sitting on a rickety bench near the backdoor of the Joint. They were, aptly, passing a joint. We slowed and I powered the window down.

"Hey guys," I said, "what kind of place is this?"

I guess they were pretty sure cops wouldn't be driving a fifty grand SUV, so one of the guys spoke.

"It sure as hell ain't no place for dudes like you."

The other guy chimed in.

"Man, this place is a shit hole but it's got broads and booze and that is all you need to make cash."

"What kind of broads?" I asked.

"What kind do you think? Whores, man. They got broads up the ass and most of them are crack whores. If you got bread, they got pussy."

"You guys work here?" Murray asked.

"No, old man, we hang around out here for the hell of it."

Murray looked at me with that "I'm going to kick some ass" look in his eye.

"You didn't tell me this was a comedy club, bro," he said, giving the wise guy his worst stink eye.

"My friend here doesn't appreciate your humor," I said. "Talk some straight shit."

The wise guy got the message.

"Yeah, we work here," he said. "We get fifty bucks to stock the coolers before opening and another fifty to keep them stocked all night."

"Where do the broads come from?" I asked. "Do they just show up?"

"Some of them do," the first guy said, "but some come in some vans. Dudes drive them up and herd 'em in."

"Herd?" I said.

"Yeah, they look like prison vans," the guy laughed. "The bouncers get out and make sure the snatch all make it into the bar."

"You look like you know a lot about prison vans," Murray said, laughing.

"Whatever," the guy said, taking a drag of the joint. He handed it to the other guy who looked at me and flipped me the bird. I thought Murman might do something retaliatory but he just smiled. He drove down the gravel path past the joint and turned right to get back on to the pavement of Exchange Street. He pulled over to the curb.

"What are you thinking?" I said.

"I think we should comeback with a flamethrower when nobody's in there and burn the shithole to the ground."

"And where would you get a flamethrower?"

Murray just smiled at me and that told me a lot more than I needed to know.

The brief look at the Loading Dock gave rise to more questions than answers but I expected that. It was time I started putting some pieces of this growing puzzle together. But I would need some more intellectual band width. Eddie dropped me off at his bar and I called Lexi from the car as I headed north.

"What's up" she asked.

"Ever heard of a place called the Loading Dock?"

"Can I call you back? I'm doing something to help out a friend and I need to concentrate on the job at hand."

"Sure. I'm heading home. You can reach me there." I needn't have added the last sentence. Lexi dropped the call as soon as I mentioned home. With her social graces, it was a good thing she was so damned beautiful. I nodded to Simon and almost made it to the elevator before he stopped me.

"Visit your mother," he said.

"Is that advice or a command?"

"Uh huh," he said with a smile. To mother's I would go. She was on the west terrace when I arrived.

"Would you like some tea, Coe?"

"Sure, if you are having some."

She came in from the terrace and made her way to the stove. She flicked on a burner and placed the kettle on it. There was a service for two on the kitchen island.

"Why don't you just nuke the water?" I said.

"My dear boy," she said, laughing, "you aren't in Mexico any longer. You can't put a Fortnum's tea cup in a microwave. Don't be in such a hurry all the time."

I sat on her couch while the water boiled and watched her pour it into a delicate-looking teapot. She pulled a box from one of the cupboards.

"What's your pleasure?" she said, surveying the box.

"Ah ... tea would be fine, Mother. I'm not a connoisseur so you pick something you like. I'm sure it will be fine."

She smiled that 'Oh Coe, you barbarian' smile and pulled a couple of packets from the box.

"What is that, exactly, Mother ... just in case the subject ever comes up." I gave her my 'oh Mother, don't be such a snob' look in return."

"It's called Smoky Earl Grey. It's a blend of black tea, oolong tea, bergamot tea, and a hint of vanilla."

"Smoky Earl Grey ... got it."

She faked a frown that turned into a smile.

"Don't try to make me feel bad because I appreciate the finer things in life.'

'I wouldn't think of it, Mother. I just find it all rather exotic after my life of simple pleasures."

"That's why you should try to upscale a bit ... to see if you like the finer things."

She brought the tea over on a silver tray and placed a cup in front of me. The cup looked too fine for me to put my lips on but I passed on the chance to tell my mother that.

She sipped hers so I did the same and, holy shit, this tea was delicious. My expression must have given my appreciation away.

"See? Sometimes the finer things are just that – finer."

We settled in and she asked what I'd discovered. I needn't ask her how she knew I was in discovery mode as she and my sister were probably in contact immediately after Sheila called me. I told her how cursory my first exploration had been and of my suspicions that something was rotten on Exchange Street.

"There are a lot of rumors circulating about that place," she said, "so it is good you aren't on camera inside the place. But I have to emphasize again the need for caution, Coe. You are dealing with the worst of the worst."

"Good thing I've got the best of the best on my team then," I said. Damn, this tea was good. I told her about Murray's flamethrower comment to lighten the mood. It didn't work.

"If Eddie brought it up, you can be sure he was playing."

"Be flip if you must, but be careful and don't be afraid to let the police handle anything nefarious – understand?"

I allowed that I would and finished my tea.

"That was the best tea ever. Where did you get that?"

"I'll order you some, Coe. Please remain in good enough health to enjoy it."

I promised her I would, kissed her cheek and headed down to my place to wait for Lexi's call.

I got back to my apartment anxious to call Lexi and let her know what Eddie and I had found out. I needn't have bothered. When I opened the door she was pumping out push-ups, first with two hands and then with alternating one-arm jobs. She barely glanced at me as she continued.

"Where the hell have you been?" she said.

"Ah, do you really need to being doing push-ups on my Australian sheepskin rug?"

"It's nice and cushiony. Don't tell me. Your mom picked it out."

She said not to tell her so I didn't. But my mother did pick it out.

"What brings you to your manic phase this evening, my lovely; a manic phase you deem necessary to indulge in my apartment? Speaking of which, how did you get in to my apartment?"

She cranked out a half dozen more push-ups and stopped.

"I told you. Your doorman has the hots for me. He was kind enough to let me up. He told me you were home so I didn't see the problem. Visiting momma again, were you?"

I needed to have a chat with Simon.

"Yes, I was. We had tea together …"

"Oh, tea? Did you hold your pinky out while sipping?" I failed to see the humor but Lexi got a big kick out of herself.

"No pinky," I said, "but the tea was extraordinary." I threw her a towel from the kitchen before her sweat sullied my rug. "So why the adrenalin rush?"

"I got to go on a stakeout," she said. "It was almost like the old days when I was a cop."

"Almost?"

Yeah. This time I didn't get to put the cuffs on anyone but I did get an eyeful of some really nefarious shit."

"Nefarious?"

"Yeah, nefarious. You aren't the only one with a dictionary."

She went on to explain that one of her old cop friends retired and took a job as an inspector general with the Buffalo office of the Department of Housing and Urban Development. This friend, one Colleen Mayer, asked Lexi to ride along while she checked out a tip that came into her office. The tip involved a bunch of guys who were hired to clean up foreclosed properties that were going to be put on the market by HUD. The crew was supposed to remove debris then board up the houses. It seems, though, they had a funny definition of "debris" as they had been seen removing anything and everything of value from the houses; a definite no-no.

"So we drive over to Black Rock and sat on a house that was scheduled for cleaning," Lexi said. "Pretty soon a van pulls up and four guys who look like they played for the Bills get out and go inside. Not ten minutes later two guys come out with the hot water tank. Then the other two guys come out carrying a toilet. Thirty minutes we watch these assholes bringing out anything not nailed down.

"All the while, Colleen is snapping pictures of the larceny. The guys go in again and are in there for a long time. I tell her to get a shot of the van and the license plate. About half an hour later, the four guys come out carrying the furnace. Can you believe that shit?"

I knew now why Lexi was so pumped up. Nothing gets her jazzed like catching bad guys and nothing frustrates her more than not being able to do anything about it.

"So then what?" I asked.

The gleam in her eye faded a little.

"So then nothing," she said. "Colleen said she would turn the photos over to the FBI and they would get to have all the fun."

I went to the refrigerator and got her a bottle of water and I joined her on the floor.

"Did you do anything fun tonight?" she asked, so I told her about the trip I made with Murray.

"The Loading Dock, huh?" she said, between gulps. "Never heard of it."

"It seems that few people have. My sister gave me a tip about the place and something definitely smells."

I shared with her the highlights of the conversation we'd had with the two stoners ending with Murman's comment about the flamethrower.

"Gotta love a man of action," she said.

"Speaking of 'action' ..." she said as she rolled on top of me.

I made a mental note to thank Lexi's friend for getting her juiced.

CHAPTER ELEVEN

I WOKE UP THINKING IT would be great to have Lexi lying next to me. But deep down, I knew better. Her side of the bed was empty as usual. Her phone call would have to suffice.

"What's on tap for today?" she said.

"I got nothing on the calendar. How about you?"

"Let's take a drive by the joint you found last night. I want to take a look at the place."

"Okay, when?"

"Right after you buy me breakfast. I'm at Pano's. Get your ass down here."

"Yes, ma'am. I'll be there in fifteen minutes."

Lexi clicked off the call. She wasn't one for lengthy goodbyes. Actually, she wasn't big on goodbyes at all. I jumped into the shower and was dressed in ten minutes. I got to Pano's in sixteen minutes.

Lexi's greeting was warm.

"You're late. You are going to have to work on your timing."

But she did kiss me hello so that was good. We ordered and while we were waiting, we talked about her night with the HUD inspector. I had had some dealings with HUD when I was the Mayor's Chief of Staff. I knew there were a lot of foreclosed houses that needed cleaning and boarding up before they went on the market. If someone emptied those houses of anything of value, they would be accumulating a lot of loot.

"You didn't follow the van, did you?" I said.

"No. We just watched them carry out the goodies and took pictures. Why?"

"You have to assume this wasn't the first house they looted. If these thieves are taking water tanks and furnaces, they have to have a pretty big place to store that stuff."

"You're right. I guess we got so pumped getting the goods on these guys we overlooked that part of it. Should I call Colleen and see if she's planning another snoop and shoot?"

"Ask her if there are other houses that might be targets. If she gives you an address or two we might be able to do our own observation and track the assholes to their storage area. Then you can give her the intel and let her take the credit for finding the stash."

"Good idea. Sometimes you amaze me, Coe Duffy."

Breakfast came and we ate in relative silence until Lexi asked about the AWOL GI.

"I haven't heard anything from anyone," I told her. "Maybe it's time we reached out to our cop buddies."

"You mean my cop buddies? When last I checked you were out of friends at police headquarters."

"Wait, what? I still have friends there."

"You mean your old boss has friends there and you can ask him to check, right?"

"Well, yeah, but they are my friends too."

I had a weak case for that claim. After Lexi arrested me and gave up her promising career as a cop to avoid testifying against me, my contacts in the department were not happy with me. Some of them still spoke to me but even that was done grudgingly.

She dismissed me with a laugh.

"I'll call around this afternoon to see if there are any developments. What are you going to do?"

"Not sure yet but you did want to do a drive by of the Loading Dock, right?"

"Yes, let's do that now. I'm interested to see the place before Murray burns it down."

I paid, as usual, and I went right to her Jeep.

"How did you know I was going to drive?" she said.

I was going to say something, but she winked at me and shut me down.

It didn't take long to hit Exchange Street and do the drive-by of the Loading Dock. It was, of course, closed at this early hour but I had Lexi make the turn to the service road at the back of the place.

"This is it?" she said.

"Yep. There's a bit more activity at night but this is it. Hardly looks like the kind of place we'd hang around but then we aren't part of the current in-crowd."

"Speak for yourself," she said. "Need I remind you I am the dance queen of the Blu Bar in Turks and Caicos?"

The vision of her dancing that cute ass off in some tropical beach bar did create an image for me but the image only earned me a punch on the arm.

"Are you perving on me dancing, you pig?"

"Perving is all I got since you didn't see fit to invite me," I said. "Do you want me to tell you what I'm imagining?"

"Keep it to yourself. "

She stopped the Jeep and before I could ask why she pointed to a series of cameras that were spaced across the back of the building.

"I didn't notice them in front of this pigsty," she said, which is saying something because she notices everything. "I suggest that we scout from the other side of those railroad tracks so we're not on film."

The tracks were seldom used these days and had a healthy growth of weeds sprouting on the track bed. We were about twenty yards from the rear entrance of the Loading Dock. We sacrificed a better view of the place for anonymity, or so I thought. Lexi produced a monocular lens from her pocket and adjusted to get the magnified image of the building.

"Not much to look at," she said. "Can't see how they stay open with one door in front and that service entrance in the rear. They have to be violating every fire ordinance in the book. Let's check their garbage."

She pointed at a line of garbage totes strung along the service road. We walked along the tracks and made a wide loop back toward the garbage. The cameras were all pointing in the opposite direction. Lexi must have seen me contemplating that fact.

"I'd be even more suspicious of this place if they were interested in protecting their trash. Let's see what we've got."

With that, she tipped the tote farthest from the building. It was filled with all the crap you might expect from bar: empty booze and wine bottles, plastic cups, napkins, and a bunch of other stuff that looked like plain and simple garbage. Lexi slipped on a rubber glove and started a closer look at the trash. She was near the bottom of the tote when she pulled up her sleeve and dipped into the mélange. She came up with a clear plastic cup with a little fluid in it and an undissolved pill of some sort.

"I'll bet you dollars to donuts this pill is Ambien," she said.

"A sleeping pill?" I'd once been prescribed Ambien to help me sleep through some troubling post-Afghanistan nightmares.

"Yep, the new date rape drug," she said. "It makes you drowsy pretty fast and impairs memory; the perfect combination for some asshole who can't get laid on his own."

Lexi carefully dumped the remaining fluid from the cup, keeping the pill stuck to the side of it.

"What now?" I said. "Should I take a picture of it?"

"Now I get this to Cat Redmond for analysis. You watch too much CSI on television. Even if this is Ambien, it wouldn't be admissible because we aren't law enforcement. What it can do is put this place on the cop radar as an establishment where some nefarious activity is likely taking place."

"'*Nefarious*'?" I said. "You really did buy a dictionary."

That got me a rather strenuous punch on the arm. We got back to the Jeep and Lexi pulled a baggy from the glove box and put the cup inside.

"Where do you want me to drop you?" she said.

"What? I can't go with you to meet Cat?"

"No, you can't. This is semi-official stuff, and you're just quasi-official."

Lexi drove me back to Pano's to get my car, then peeled off heading for police headquarters, leaving me to wonder what the hell was going on.

I went home and called Murray to let him know what we'd found.

"Sleeping pills? These bastards are doping girls with sleeping pills? We need to start kicking some ass in that place. This is bullshit."

"Indeed it is, Mur," I said. "I'll let you know what Lexi finds out from the police lab but I'm feeling pretty confident that either us or the cops will be paying a visit to the Loading Dock real soon."

No sooner had I hung up with Eddie when Simon buzzed me from downstairs.

"Mr. Duffy, I have a guy down here who would like to see you," he said, "but he looks a little scruffy and appears like he was beaten by Mike Tyson. Should I send him away?"

"Did he give you a name, Simon?"

"Norton. Mr. Duffy. His name is Ron Norton."

"Don't send him away, Simon, send him up."

I opened the door to await the AWOL GI but was a little surprised when he stepped off the elevator. He was scruffy, as advertised, but he looked like he'd gone a few rounds with Mike Tyson and his evil twin. It had been a while since I'd seen anyone that lumped up.

"Mr. Duffy?" he said.

"That's me. You must be Ron Norton, of the 10th Mech?"

"That's me, at least it was me. I'm not sure it is me anymore."

"It looks like you could sit down for a while. Come on in."

The soldier walked a little wobbly into the apartment. I took his arm and put it around me to steady him as I walked him to the couch. He collapsed more than he sat, and I thought he might pass out. I laid him down and took off his shoes. He was losing the fight to keep his eyes open, so I put a throw pillow under his head. His left eye was completely swollen shut. He had a lump on the left side of his head that had bled recently. His jaw was bruised and his lip split. I glanced at his hands and saw they were scrapped and bleeding.

At least he put up a fight, I thought.

I wasn't sure what to do with this poor guy but I knew I had to do something, so I called my mother.

"Hey, you know that Norton girl you told me about?"

"Yes, Coe, I remember."

"I don't have anything on her, but her brother is passed out on my couch and he's in a real bad way. Somebody or a couple of somebodies have put a pretty heavy beating on him."

"I'll be right there," she said and almost before I heard the click of the phone, I heard the knock on my door.

Marsha came in and took one look at the guy and started punching numbers on her phone. She gave someone named Gretchen the few details we had about Ron Norton and insisted she was needed "straight away."

"No, my son's apartment ... same building, two floors below mine. The doorman will give you the information, but you must hurry."

"Marsha, this guy is AWOL and looking for his sister. We aren't getting the cops in on this, are we?"

"No, Coe, Gretchen retired from medical practice and has always been helpful in situations like this."

I wondered how many "situations like this" my mother encountered that needed the help of a physician but thought better of asking.

"Help me lift up his shirt. I need to see if there are any more injuries."

As soon as we started to lift the shirt, he moaned. We got the shirt over his ribs and saw the deep purple bruising over his ribs. She said it as I was thinking it:

"He's probably got some internal injuries worse than those on his face."

And his face was a mess.

I had to assume Doc Gretchen lived close by as she was knocking on my door in less than ten minutes. Marsha hugged her as she entered and thanked her for coming so quickly. Then she went to the couch and the badly beaten man. She made a face when she saw his torso. She lifted one eyelid and then the other, shining a small light into each eye. She touched his swollen cheek, then the battered jaw. She took a stethoscope from a small bag she brought with her and listened to Norton's heart, then turned to my mother.

"I know this isn't what you want to hear, Marsha, but the boy needs a hospital," she said. "I'm pretty sure he has a concussion and some badly broken ribs. I think he might have a zygomatic fracture in his cheek and the ribs might have caused some internal damage. I couldn't be sure just by looking at the injuries, but you can tell there was extreme force like kicking that broke those ribs. He needs to be more closely examined quickly."

Marsha hugged the doctor and thanked her as she walked her to the door. Not many moms have doctors on call like this and I couldn't guess how many times she needed to make such a call, but I was glad she did. I remembered what Father Ryan had said about layers. Apparently, my father wasn't the only one with layers. My wonder continued as I heard the siren getting closer. I looked at her, but she assured me it wasn't a Marsha miracle.

"Gretchen called for the ambulance," she said. "She's retired but still very connected."

The siren stopped a few minutes later and the crew was at my door and collecting one beat-all-to-hell soldier for their stretcher.

"Where will you be taking him?" Marsha asked.

One of the EMTs called back over his shoulder.

"We're taking him to ECMC. They have the best trauma unit around. That was Dr. Broderick's order."

She nodded and that fast, Ron Norton was on his way to the elevator and on his way to far better treatment than he could have gotten on my couch.

"Did he say anything to you?" Marsha asked.

"He could barely stand when he got off the elevator," I told her. "I haven't seen anyone beaten that bad in a long, damned time."

"I was thinking the same thing," she said. "Gretchen knows when I call, I'm asking for her discretion so her recommending a hospital means our young soldier was in trouble. I'm guessing his search for his sister had something to do with his beating.

"How did he know to contact you?"

"I gave my card to his dad after assuring the old man I wasn't an AWOL hunter. I'm glad he trusted me enough to come here. You are probably right about what got him beaten but I can tell you without much hesitation that some son of a bitch is going to pay for this."

"Don't let your anger cloud your judgment," Marsha said. "If you want to help the boy, you need a clear head."

I hated it when she was right and rational when I was pissed off and impulsive, but I knew she was right – again.

"I'll check with Dr. Broderick tomorrow and see when we might be able to talk to the lad," she said. "It will probably take a day or two unless he needs surgery and then it might be a week."

I was too mad to talk so I merely nodded. She came close and hugged me.

"Don't do anything stupid," she reminded me. "We need to be thoughtful and disciplined."

Great, I thought, thoughtful and disciplined didn't have any space on my resume but I hugged her back.

"Nothing stupid," I said, and this time my fingers weren't crossed. "I promise."

She kissed my forehead and went out the door. I promised nothing stupid, but I felt like doing something, which usually involved me being stupid. No one deserved that kind of beating but a soldier was something bordering on sacred to me. I hadn't lied when I said someone was going to pay. I was still fuming when Lexi called. I jump-started our conversation with my recap of my meeting with Ron Norton. I probably shouldn't have. She was as pissed as I was.

"We need to find out who did this and inflict some serious payback!" she shouted into the phone.

"Agreed, Lexi, but we don't know who to pay back ... yet, anyway. But we will."

She took a breath and told me about Detective Redmond taking the pill Lexi had found for analysis. Then she told me about the call from Colleen Mayer. She asked Lexi if she would like to sit on another house that was scheduled for a "cleaning." Of course, Lexi was in, and she wanted me along for the ride. I needed something to take my mind of PFC Norton, so I told her to pick me up. Twenty minutes later, Simon buzzed me and told me: "your chick is here." I told him it was okay to call her that when speaking to me but if "the chick" ever heard him say that he would need an orthodontist. He was smiling when I started to climb in the Jeep. I looked at him coldly.

"I wasn't fucking around," I said, and his smile disappeared.

We pulled away and Lexi looked at me.

"What was that all about?"

"Just boy talk. You wouldn't be interested." Oddly enough, that seemed to satisfy her.

"Where are we heading this afternoon?" I asked.

"Some house on the eastern border of the city," she said. "I hate it when all we get to do is watch."

"That's the cop in you," I said. "You'll get used to it."

Her smirk told me she was nowhere near that point now. It didn't take long until we were in a maze of streets lined with small, well-groomed yards and neat houses. We travelled down the block, and I spotted the target house immediately and not because I was so observant. The front lawn was about two feet high and littered with trash. The house looked like it hadn't been painted in years. This was the foreclosure, and they all looked the same, no matter what the neighborhood. We parked five houses forward of the house.

"The cleaners are due here at four," Lexi said, "and they are always on time. We have about ten minutes."

It was more like seven minutes when the non-descript white panel van pulled in front of the target house; non-descript except that it was a Mercedes.

"Damn, cleaning these ghost houses must pay well," I said.

"That's a different van than I saw before," Lexi said. "I hope these are the same guys."

It didn't take long before she recognized the crew, and they were as burly as advertised.

"Those are some big dudes," I said.

"Told you." she said. "Wait till you see them in action."

It only took a few minutes before the monsters were carrying out everything that wasn't bolted down: toilets, sinks, appliances, the works.

"Something tells me those items are not part of the deal," I said, as Lexi snapped away with her Canon EOS M50.

Thirty minutes later, the van drove off. I suggested that Lexi follow.

"We know what they're doing," I said, "but we might find out where they store the stuff. The more you give your HUD buddy the better."

"I knew I brought you along for a reason," she said, but I still got the punch on the arm.

We followed the van for about twenty minutes along the Lake Erie shoreline and into the remains of the former Bethlehem Steel plant. It pulled up to a decrepit building that once might have been a warehouse but now looked like a candidate for demolition. We stopped behind another skeleton of a building and watched. The gorillas got out of the van and started carrying their booty into the building. I was amazed by their strength. One guy carried two toilets like they were infant children. Another guy had a hot water tank on his shoulder and a bathroom sink in his hand.

"Those are some strong-assed dudes," I said.

"We've beat better," Lexi said, and I tried to remember if we ever did and when that might have happened.

"Good thing we're just here to observe," I said, truly meaning it.

Lexi just smiled in response.

CHAPTER TWELVE

WE PULLED OUT OF THE decrepit plant and headed back north. Lexi said she was going to share our new knowledge with her HUD contact, and I wanted an update on Ron Norton. Lexi dropped me off with Simon nowhere in sight. Maybe he took my warning seriously. For his sake, I hoped he had. I took the elevator straight to Marsha's apartment. She was on the phone when she let me in.

"Thank you, Doctor," she said into the phone. "I appreciate you keeping me updated." Then she put the phone down and hugged me like she's never hugged me before.

"What's this all about, Marsha? You just happy to see me?"

"Of course I am, Coe, you fool! I saw what happened to that poor boy and all I could think of was you in that sad shape. You keep sticking your nose into all this crap and see what the results are?"

"If you think I am going to simply walk away having seen what someone did to that kid, you are crazy, Marsha. Speaking of which, I have to call his parents and let them know what's happened to their son. Can we take care of some of the costs for treating the kid. It's the only way we can keep the MPs off his ass for a while."

"Neither you nor the boy's family has to worry about that, Coe. I was just on the phone with the medical director of the hospital. You needn't tell the boy's parents that."

It was my turn. I hugged her for all I was worth and was glad she couldn't see the tear leaking out of my eye.

"Marsha, you are a truly wonderful woman."

She pulled away just far enough to kiss my cheek.

"See what you've gotten me into?" she said. Then she smiled. "Go call the Nortons and let them know their son is in good hands. We'll work on getting his sister in good hands straightaway."

And somehow, I knew we would.

"Mr. Norton, Ron is in good hands, I can assure you. He took quite a beating but he's a soldier, so he'll be OK. Thank you for giving him my card. Him showing up here was a surprise but he came to the right place."

The father thanked me after I told him the phone numbers at ECMC. My next call was to Moe in D.C. I explained what had happened and where the PFC was for the next week or so.

"Can you get the Army to cool their jets for a while on this?" I asked. "Fuck, Moe, if it was easy, I wouldn't need you, would I? The kid took a great big ass-kicking looking for his twin sister. See if you can get a little goodwill from your former employers. Tell them to call me if they need more information. Yeah, I know they would just as soon lock me up as talk to me. That was a little humor among old grunts. Thanks, Moe, I owe you big time for this one."

I didn't know if there was a damned thing Moe could do to keep the GI hounds at bay, but I was hoping he could pull something out of his hat. PFC Ron Norton had enough going on without having to worry about being hauled off in handcuffs. But we were still facing the missing sister. But if my mom was going to be part of the pursuit, we would be in good hands. I got a bottle of Perrier and went out on the terrace. The sky was bleeding its final red rays of the sun behind Lake Erie. The early night sky was darkening from navy blue to black. The beauty of this view, the terrace I viewed it from, the mother I'd only recently discovered, the woman that drove me crazy ... my life had turned a hundred and eighty degrees from being paid by the base hit in the Mexican Pro League. But even in this great turnabout,

I was still confronting the demons that seemed to be everywhere around me. Maybe after this escapade, I could relax … but who was I kidding?

I didn't have much time to ponder that as my phone buzzed with a call from Ed Murray.

"Hey, Mur, what's up?"

"That's what I was calling about. What's going on?"

I filled him in on the surveillance we conducted for HUD and where that took us. I saved the Norton story for last because I knew what Eddie's reaction would be. He wanted to arm up and prowl the streets until we found the guys responsible for Norton's beating.

I was in the process of calming him down long enough to let him know I felt the same way he did when another call buzzed.

"Eddie, I'll let you know when we get targets. You know I wouldn't leave you out of payback but Lexi's on the other line, so I have to go."

"Hey," Murray said, "don't you and your girl go out and find these assholes without me."

"I promise, Ed. You will be my first call …"

I ended that call and jumped on with Lexi.

"How did your meet with the HUD gal go? Was she impressed we cracked her case for her?"

"Of course she was impressed, although she did yell at me for taking unnecessary risks."

"I'm sure you took that like a good team player," I laughed.

"What are we doing for dinner?" she said.

"What do you want? You want to come over here or go out? I'm not really wanting to get duded up for a date."

"Duded up? When in the hell did you ever get duded up to take me out?"

She had a point.

"I'll order from the seafood joint down the street from me," she said. "You are responsible for the wine."

"I can do that," I said, knowing that my mother would have exactly the right wine for fish.

"Hey, why don't you ask your mother to join us? I know you would have to call her about the wine so just have her come down to your place. I still haven't thanked her for the help she was on the Central Terminal deal."

Sweet Lexi had no clue how much "help" my mother provided when we found the treasure and she wouldn't ever find out from me. Lexi was convinced that it was our expert sleuthing that led us to the jackpot, and I wasn't ever going to detract from that. Truth was we'd still be searching all over town for the lost loot if not for Marsha.

"Great idea ... again," I said. "I'll call her now. When do you think you'll be here?"

"More like another great idea," she said. "Give me ninety minutes."

We hung up and I called my mother with the invitation.

"Why Coe, how sweet of Lexi to include me. I was beginning to think you were ashamed of me," she said.

"Why do you assume it was Lexi's idea?" I said.

"Because all the best ideas come from us women." She definitely had me there.

"What wine do you think I should serve?" I said. "Lexi' is bringing something from that seafood place on Ellicott Street."

"You might have asked her what she had in mind, but they have wonderful tuna and some exquisite sea bass. Look in your rack and take a bottle of Goldeneye Pinot Noir out. There should also be a nice Chateau de La Perriere Brouilly. Why don't you uncork that and let it breathe? I trust you two will be casual?"

"Yep. We decided to eat in and not dress up for dinner."

"Coe, when did you ever dress up for dinner?" She giggled and hung up. What was it with the women in my life all thinking the same thoughts about me dressing up? I'll show them, I thought, and went into the bedroom to get a clean pair of khakis.

An hour or so later, Simon told me I had a delivery of "something that smelled like heaven itself." I wasn't sure what that might be but when I opened the door, I knew exactly what he meant. A fellow dressed in white was wheeling a serving cart with a spiffy looking food warmer on it. I thought Lexi was bringing the food, but the deliveryman said that once the chef knew that Marsha McCartan would be dining, he insisted the food be kept hot. That's my mom. She was known and loved everywhere. I was worried that Lexi might not take it well if her efforts were upstaged by the chef, but she came in right behind the food to make sure I had set the right table.

"God, it smells divine, doesn't it?" she said.

"What did you get? That serving thingy looks like it has food for an entire platoon."

"I told the chef I wanted to impress someone, and he asked who. When I told him, he went into a tizzy. So we have some sea bass, some tuna, and a slab of swordfish, just in case."

"Just in case what?" I said.

"I don't know. That's what the chef said."

It was only then did I noticed how absolutely stunning Lexi looked. Her dark hair was pulled back revealing her flawless skin and incredible face. She was not a fan of a lot of make-up but what she used, she used quite well. She was wearing a white shirt over her jeans and sandals. The shirt highlighted the remaining glow of her Caribbean tan. In short, she looked as good as the food smelled. She caught me staring at her and gave me one of those looks that inferred "I told you I was worth it."

I might have done something rash if Marsha had not arrived at that instant. She was a beautiful woman made more beautiful by the simplicity with which she dressed and carried herself. Her hair was perfectly coiffed, and her cashmere sweater was of a shade that highlighted her skin tone. She too wore nicely tailored jeans. Her Aigner loafers were shining up from the floor. I wondered what I'd done to warrant two such stunning and accomplished women in my life. Marsha took an exaggerated whiff of the delightful aromas and looked at me.

"Don't just stand there staring at Lexi," she said. "Introduce us."

I realized that after all this time that Lexi and I had been an item, then not an item, then perhaps an item, she and Marsha had never met. I took Lexi's hand.

"Marsha, meet Lexi Crane. Lexi, this is my mother, Marsha McCartan."

Lexi reached out for Marsha's hand but was soon wrapped up in a hug.

"Lexi, it is wonderful to finally meet you. Coe had told me so little about you."

That left me embarrassed as hell, mostly because it was true. I had kept two of the three most extraordinary women in my life separate and apart.

"That ends tonight," I said, trying most to convince myself. I poured three glasses of wine and raised my glass.

"To women with beauty, brains, and intelligence ..." I started.

Marsha cut in with "... and to the men smart enough to recognize all three."

With that we sat to enjoy the sumptuous spread laid out on the table. The serving sizes were big enough that we could share all three entrees.

"Marsha, your selection of the wines is perfect," Lexi said, purposefully ignoring me.

Marsha looked to me and smiled.

"Thank you, Lexi. I'm always glad to help when Coe needs a little help with the selections. Wine isn't exactly his thing."

"With you holding the cue cards, Coe makes some really great selections," Lexi said.

"Coe's tastes run along the same lines as his father, I'm afraid. He has a wonderfully refined palate for lagers."

If the women thought that might embarrass me, they were wrong.

"I like what I like," I said, between bites, as I reached out for both of their hands.

We ate while Lexi and Marsha got acquainted; Lexi detailing her teenage years as one of the state's finest female athletes, her father's untimely death in an armed robbery, and her decision to forego college for a career in law enforcement. I had the feeling Marsha knew all this but she sat attentively, nonetheless.

"You are a wonderfully accomplished woman, Lexi," she said, "but I do wish you had gone on to college. Your devotion to law enforcement is understandable and laudable, given the circumstances of you father's untimely death. A career in law might have been an acceptable alternative."

"I am only two semesters short of my bachelor's degree in criminal justice," Lexi said, "and law school might be a possibility."

I tried not to look surprised. I had no idea Lexi was going to school. I guess that's part of the feminine mystique I'd heard about. Upon my first return from my self-imposed exile in Mexico, I'd learned that Lexi could sing and that she was a frequent performer at my friend Dennis Talty's pub. Clearly, there was a lot about this woman I could stand to learn, and I smiled when I thought of Father Ryan's comment about my dad and his layers. We were almost finished with dinner when Lexi let out a shriek.

"Oh my God," she shouted. "I completely forgot about dessert!"

"Are you kidding?" I said. "If I eat another bite I'll need new pants."

"Lexi, the meal was divine and you needn't fret about dessert," Marsha said.

We cleared the table, wrapped the leftovers, and headed out to the terrace for some coffee. Before we got there, Simon was on the intercom.

"Coe, you've got a visitor," he said.

"Who is it?"

"They insist on secrecy."

"Well, are they friend or foe?"

"Let me put it this way: if this visitor was my friend, I'd be a happy dude."

"Let them in."

A minute later, the third person in my trinity of extraordinary women knocked on the door. There was my half-sister, Sheila, with a carrot cake big enough that it needed two hands to hold.

"I hope I'm not intruding," she said, kissing me on the cheek. She was stunning, her aura wafting with her signature scent, Beautiful, and her face radiant with a touch of perspiration. (I'd learned from Lexi that women don't sweat, they perspire.) But her presence made me self-conscious again for not having had the foresight to invite her. I took the cake from her and she went to the terrace to hug, first, Marsha, then Lexi.

"It is so nice to finally put a face to the name," Sheila said. "I can see why Coe always gets red in the face when he talks about you."

"And you must be Sheila," Lexi said. "I'm glad you are related to Coe otherwise I would be very jealous of how much he admires you."

I wondered if the women knew I was standing right there.

"Sheila, help me cut some of this cake. We were just lamenting someone had forgotten all about dessert when you saved the day," I said.

As we walked back to the kitchen, I whispered my regrets at having been an ass and not inviting her to dinner.

"No worries, Coe. I couldn't have made it anyway. My presence was required at the Birchfield-Penny Art Gallery. But mother thought you might like the cake."

I put the cake down and hugged her tight.

"I can't believe that three such incredible women are in my life."

She hugged me back and said softly "we're the lucky ones."

Sheila cut the cake and I carried it out to the terrace. When everyone was served and coffee and tea poured, my mother surprised the hell out of me.

"Dinner was lovely and the dessert looks scrumptious but let's talk about what needs to be said."

"What might that be, Marsha?" I said.

"We have a young man lying in a hospital bed beaten within an inch of his life," she said. "His only crime, as I see it, was looking for his missing twin sister. We will allow doctors to tend to the soldier but we must fulfill his mission and find his sister." She paused long enough to sip her tea and continued.

"What do we know, Coe? And Lexi, that includes you. Feel free to jump in at any time."

I started with my chance meeting with the scraggly girl on Elmwood Avenue and her bullshit story about looking for the woman who turned out to be Jennifer Norton. I continued with my effort to find out about a GI who might have ill-will toward the girl and discovered that the searcher was, in fact, Jennifer's twin brother. I gave Marsha a glance to let her know she was up.

"Yes, and my contacts determined that Jennifer Norton was a nursing student and waitress and had been looking for a couple of younger co-workers who seemed to be missing. As a result of her tenacity, she is now missing."

It was Sheila's turn. She told how she had filled me in on the new nightspot called the Loading Dock. I was about to relate the recon Eddie Murray and I did at the Loading Dock, but Lexi jumped in with her piece about finding the largely intact pill that a BPD lab determined to be Ambien. I took a bite of the carrot cake while Lexi spoke, and it was extraordinary. When Lexi stopped, I realized I was the only one eating. Lexi shot me a disapproving look and commented.

"When should we go looking for those new pants?"

We had the catalogue of where we'd all been and now needed to plot where we were going.

My mother took charge like a battlefield commander.

"Lexi, might you use your police contacts to see if there are any reports regarding the Loading Dock? Sheila, you can mine your contacts as well to see what goes on at that place. If they are dosing girls, there's no telling what else they are doing. Coe, you and I will go to the hospital to learn what we can about what happened to that young man, where it happened, and upon whom we might exact some revenge."

Everyone nodded approval and then they started on the dessert. When everyone had eaten, I started clearing the dishes and my mother joined me. We made it to the kitchen sink when I asked her what she'd done with my mother, the one who had chastised me severely about sticking my noise into the doings of the scum who might entrap Buffalo girls.

"Coe, there are times when good people have to stand up. You know that from your time in southwest Asia. You know that from your adventures with that delightful Lexi in solving the mystery at Central Terminal. You can sense it now when you saw what happened to the Norton fellow who is looking to find his sister. This kind of thuggery can't be allowed to stand in our community; not if we have anything to say about it. We're going to help this young man and we're going to be quick about it."

I put down the handful of plates I carried and gave her the biggest hug we'd yet shared.

"You are a hell of a woman," I whispered.

"You ain't seen nothing yet, kid." Then she kissed me and said her good-byes to Lexi. She had Sheila by the arm when they went to my door. Sheila broke away long enough to kiss my cheek.

"We're going to find this girl," she said. "Mother never fails."

When they had left, Lexi helped me take care of the dishes, then we retired to the sofa.

"That was some hug you gave your mother," she said. "Did she give you another stock tip or something?"

"Nope, she just surprised the hell out of me the way she injected herself in our mission and took charge. She wasn't happy when I came back from Mexico and told her what I'd been doing down there."

"So," Lexi said, "you like women who take charge, do you?" Then she straddled my lap and took charge.

CHAPTER THIRTEEN

I WAS WAKENED BY the buzz of my cell phone. It was Marsha.

"Are you alone?" she asked.

"Yep, Lexi never stays the night. She is obsessive about sleeping in her own bed."

"Well, get cleaned up. We can go see Private Norton at ten."

It was a minute to ten when she knocked. I had thrown on a Bills t-shirt and some jeans and my trusty Adidas. Marsha, on the other hand, looked like she'd spent all night getting ready: perfectly coiffed and impeccably dressed.

"Did you call the doctor?" I said. "It's OK we talk to Norton?"

"The doctor called me this morning," she said. "He said the lad was still healing but he was awake and responsive."

Marsha's Mercedes was already in front and Simon was holding the door.

"Thank you, Simon. Coe will take care of your gratuity later."

It took less than ten minutes to get to ECMC, the Erie County Medical Center. The facility had grown from a public hospital into the premier trauma center in the region with enough ancillary services to transform it from a hospital to a campus of related buildings. We checked at the entry desk and were met shortly thereafter by a nurse who led us to the head injury unit. As soon as we got off the elevator, we were met by a man whose name tag identified him as Dr. DeNoble.

"Marsha, it is a pleasure to see you again," the doc said, taking her hand.

"You also, Doctor. How's our patient?"

"He sustained quite a beating," the doctor said. "He has a pretty deep head wound but minimal signs of concussive symptoms. His worst injury is an orbital fracture on his right cheek near the nose. We have determined the nose isn't broken although it is quite swollen. There has been some hemorrhaging in the right eye and when you see him the redness in the eyeball itself is reflective of that bleeding. Our ophthalmic specialists don't think surgery is necessary. We used seventeen stitches to close his head wound and another nine to close a wound on the cheek. He has some swelling on the right side of the jaw but no impairment of speech and no indication of fracture. He has two fractured fingers, presumably from having punched something hard, and finally, he has two broken ribs. In summary, someone beat this boy badly."

The more the doctor spoke, the angrier I got. I didn't think one guy would have inflicted this kind of damage and the hand fractures told me the kid fought back, at least while he could. I was still amazed that he could have made it to my place in that condition.

"Might we speak with him?" Marsha said.

"Of course, but he might tire rather quickly. As I said, he's been through a lot."

Marsha took the doctor's hand in both of hers and said something I couldn't hear. He nodded and left.

"What did you say?" I said.

"I was just telling him where the hospital could send the bill." She got a kiss from me for that.

We entered the room. Norton was sitting almost upright in his bed. He had the ubiquitous IV drip but that was about the only thing that looked normal. I'd seen guys messed up in combat, but this guy was a different kind of messed up. His stitches were new and raw. His head had been shaved around the wound in his scalp and his entire face looked bruised and swollen. He looked at me with one eye swollen shut.

"Mr. Duffy, hello. Thanks for coming to see me."

"Hello Ronnie. This is my mom, Marsha McCartan. This is partly a friendly visit and partly a discovery visit. We're trying to find out who did this to you. Can you answer a few questions?"

Norton looked agitated, which was not what I wanted to do to him.

"I'll try, Mr. Duffy, but I might not be much help. I didn't know the guys who hit me, and I only saw two of them."

My mother moved to the chair at his bedside and took his good hand in hers.

"Ronnie … may I call you Ronnie?"

"'Course, ma'am."

"Well, Ronnie, can you tell us how this happened. Where were you? We assume you were searching for your sister Jennifer."

Her hand was working some kind of magic as the boy let go of the tension I'd seen gripping him.

"Yes, ma'am, I was. One of Jenny's friends called Ft. Knox and got a message to me that she was missing. I was going to go through the right process to get leave but I thought it would take too long so I just left. I'm in trouble, ain't I?"

"Nothing we can't fix," I said. "But first, we're going to help you get better. In the meantime, we're going to look for Jennifer also. We need whatever you can tell us to start looking."

The kid looked like he'd been put through a spin cycle on an industrial washing machine but for the next five minutes he spoke without taking a breath. He told us he'd gone to the Chippewa Street Strip to try to trace his sister's steps or to, at least, talk to someone who might have seen her. He said a bouncer at a place on the Strip told him he had seen the girl and remembered because she was looking for her lost friend. The bouncer told him asking questions was not the way to make friends in the neighborhood but before Norton walked away, the guy told him that the Loading Dock might be the place to look. So Norton took an Uber to the place. It was early evening, and the place wasn't open yet. A guy stocking coolers told him to come back after ten when the place opened. Norton then walked back to the Arena district and waited till the appointed hour, then walked back to the Loading Dock. He said the place was rocking with loud music and flashing lights but he got to talk to someone who said he was the manager. Norton described him as "a boxcar big dude" and I started wondering if I'd already seen this guy at a warehouse schlepping hot water tanks. The manager told Norton to meet him in the back behind the place where they could talk. The kid walked around back to find the manager and two more gorillas. He said he thought the manager guy was legitimate and he wasn't expecting the reception he got. The manager said, "let me see that picture again" and when Norton showed it to him one of the other guys sucker punched him in the face. Norton said the blow staggered him, but he didn't go down. Instead, he faked being really hurt and he bent low and away from the attackers. One guy came in to land another punch, but Norton said he punched him hard in the balls and when the guy bent over, he landed a solid upper cut that knocked the guy back a few steps. Another guy came at him and Norton said he landed a pretty right hand but the guy wasn't fazed.

"I knew I was toast, though," he said. "I knew my hand was broken and I'm not too good with my left."

It was then he got hit over the head from behind and "the lights went out."

"When I came to, I didn't know where I was. I was lying alongside some railroad tracks, and I knew from walking to and from the place that tracks ran into downtown so I walked along the tracks until I hit a little train station. I had called my dad and he told me to call you if I needed help. I wrote down the phone number and address. There were a bunch of cabs there so I gave one of them the address and the next thing I knew the driver was shaking me awake and said we were there ... I mean, here ... at your building, you know."

"Is this Jennifer's picture?" I said, lifting it off the GI's nightstand.

"Yep. It was just lying there next to me, so I picked it up. Didn't seem right to just leave her in the dirt."

The soldier's eyes were struggling to stay open, and I figured we got as much out of him as we could. Marsha stroked his hair, and his eyes gave up the fight. While she tended to Norton, I palmed the picture and slid it into my pocket.

As we left the room, I told my mother about the surveillance work Lexi and I had done for the HUD IG.

"It sounds like the guys stripping the houses are connected with this shithole on Exchange Street," I said.

"You might be correct, Coe," Marsha said, "but we need to strategize our next steps to make sure you are right."

I nodded my assent, but in my mind I was strategizing how Eddie Murray and I could fuck the place and a few managers up.

"Coe Duffy, you have that look in your eye that says you are about to do something stupid."

"No, Marsha. Nothing stupid, I promise."

The look she gave me indicated she didn't believe a word I'd said.

"Really, mother, nothing stupid." I would be smart about it.

•••

When we got back to West Ferry the first phone call I made was to Maloney in the Pentagon, explaining PFC Norton's plight.

"Jesus, Coe," he said. "What's going on up there? I thought the only violence you guys got involved in was watching the Bills."

"I'm not sure myself, Moe, but I damned sure am going to find out."

"Great," he said. "I make the over and under on the number of stitches you get at fifteen. As for the AWOL, I'll see what I can do."

"Thanks, buddy. I'll take the under on the number of stitches."

I hung up and called Murray.

"You going to be around for a while?" I said.

"Here all day, pal. Come on out and I'll buy you a beer."

Thirty minutes later, I pulled into Shaughnessy's parking lot. Thirty-five minutes later, I could just about see the steam coming out of Murray's ears.

"They beat that soldier like that, those rotten sonsabitches? Somebody's got to pay for that."

"Agreed," I said. "Here's what I'm thinking …"

It didn't take much to get Eddie on board. It took even less to get two of his bouncers, both UB Bull football players, to enlist in the campaign.

"We go tonight," I said. "About eleven. I'll meet you guys here and we'll ride together." A group handshake sealed the deal.

•••

Lexi was kicking the shit out of the heavy bag when the phone rang. She was going to let it go to voicemail until she saw the number.

"Hey LIndsay, how's it going girl?"

"Hi Sweetie. Thought I'd give you a heads-up. The cops driving through the Elmwood Village just called. You remember that kid you told me about, the one looking for the woman supposedly being tracked by a GI?"

"Yeah, I remember. Coe told me she fed him a line of shit about the woman being stalked by her GI boyfriend."

"She have purple hair?"

"Yeah, I think Coe mentioned that … and a bunch of piercings."

"Well, she's walking the strip today. Thought you'd want to know."

"Thanks, babe. I'll let Coe know."

Lexi took off her gloves, toweled some of the sweat off her face and dialed Coe but the call went straight to voice mail.

"Hey, give me a call I think that young chick you call Dora has surfaced. Let me know what you want to do."

Lexi got in her Jeep and headed for home when Lindsaycalled again.

"Lexi, I got off shift and thought I'd check this kid out myself. She's making her way up and down Elmwood handing something out to people. You want to meet me?"

"Hell, yeah. I can't get a hold of Coe. Where are you?"

"Elmwood and Lafayette."

"Be there in ten."

Never deemed a careful driver, Lexi made it in seven minutes and spotted Lindsay's car. She pulled up behind and walked to the car.

"Damn, girl," Lindsay said. "Have you been swimming?"

Lexi laughed. "No, I was in the gym when you called. I didn't think I had time to shower."

Then Lindsay pointed to a girl walking down Elmwood Avenue.

"That your girl?" she asked.

"Looks like it could be but without Coe I can't be sure. Let's go see what shit she's peddling."

They walked on the opposite side of the street and caught glances of the girl as she approached passers-by. Then they sped up and got ahead of her before crossing the street and walking back toward her.

"You two fine looking ladies look like you could use a night out," Dora said. "Try this club. It's got great music and some fine men hanging around." Then she handed Lexi a card that simply said THE LOADING DOCK and the address.

"Thanks," Lexi said, "but you look a little young to be hanging around a night club."

"Young, my ass," Dora said. "I'm twenty-one."

"No offense," Lexi said. "I remember when being called young was a compliment."

Dora gave her the stink eye and spat on the sidewalk.

"I hope to hell that's the chick Coe is looking for," Lindsay said. "I'd love to kick her ass and teach her some manners."

As they two women walked back to their cars, Lexi told her friend about the recon she and Coe had done at the Loading Dock and the pill that police lab determined was Ambien.

"That shit drives me crazy," Lindsay said. "Limp-dicked assholes can't get laid on their own so they think it's okay to dose a woman. We have got to check this place out and maybe kick some ass."

"I agree," Lexi said, "but we'll wait till I hear from Coe to see what he wants to do, Thanks, Lindsay. You're a doll." The two hugged and headed off.

Lexi called Coe but it went straight to voice mail.

"Call me. We've made some progress with the Loading Dock."

She got home, jumped in the shower expecting to hear from Coe. When she didn't, she lay down on her couch and drifted off to sleep.

CHAPTER FOURTEEN

I HAD SOME TIME TO kill so I headed over to the Lake Erie shoreline to visit a pal who owned Charlie's Boatyard. The place is aptly named as it overlooks the marina that docks a hundred or so boats. It was a beautiful day to take in the lake breeze and the shimmering water. I sat in an Adirondack chair and sipped my beer. I was only halfway through the beer when Chuck, the owner, showed up with another one. On a pleasant day like this it would be easy to sit here and have a puss full of Budweiser, but I had things to do this night and I needed a clear head.

"Hey Chuck, you ever heard of a place called the Loading Dock?" I asked him.

"Never been there but have heard some nasty shit about it. A couple of my regulars stopped in there a month or so ago and said they felt lucky to get out in one piece."

"Really? I heard the place was shady but didn't hear it was dangerous."

"Well, it's hearsay, like I said, but these guys said they had some money missing from the bar and when they said something to the bartender, he got pissy with them. They didn't like that but when a couple of giant bouncers showed up, they thought it best to forget about the money and head for the door. They said the bouncers followed them out to the parking lot. One of my guys carries and he thought it wise to let the muscle know that. He pulled up his shirt to show them his piece but one of the goons pulled back his jacket and showed this big-assed revolver. My buddy is a gun guy and he said it was a Ruger Red Hawk something. He said the damned thing fires a bullet bigger than a .45 so they beat a hasty retreat."

"Your guys say what the goon looked like?" I asked.

"Why, you aiming to go over there and draw down on him?" Chuck was smiling but stopped when he saw I wasn't. "No, they just said he was the only one wearing a sport coat. The other guys had muscle shirts on."

Chuck touched my arm and looked at me with a serious frown.

"Really, Coe, you aren't thinking of going over there and starting any shit, are you? My buddies aren't crazy tough, but they can hold their own and they were pretty shaken up when they got back here. They said they didn't even want to drive by the place."

I laughed. "Hell no, Chuck. I ain't going over there and starting anything. I'm just getting the lay of the land."

"Good. You spend too much money around here for you to get whacked. I've got to get back to the kitchen. Take care of yourself and come back with Lexi for dinner soon."

I shook Chuck's hand and sipped the cold Bud while watching the sun sink behind the Canadian shoreline. My friend had given me some important intelligence. Now, I needed to figure out what to do with it. I didn't like the knowledge the bad guys had guns. I have an aversion to firearms that results from my semi-successful southwest Asia adventure in Afghanistan. Thus far, I haven't encountered situations that needed a gun and I wasn't sure this one would necessitate one but I texted the new information to Murray. I know he'd be carrying and would have no hesitation to use a gun if needed. I sat in the deepening darkness and formulated the plan of attack. It's good to have a plan but it's better to know that in the first fury of violence plans tend to go all to hell. So reaction was more important than planning in my experience. It wouldn't be much of a plan anyway. I was counting on the goons to use the same tactics they employed with Ronnie Norton. But Ronnie didn't have backup. I took a walk along the shoreline bike path and let the night swallow me up. I got the familiar tingling that always accompanied the lead up to action for me. Then it was time to go. I drove out to Eddie's place and he and his guys were in the parking lot. One of them was smacking an aluminum baseball bat into his open palm. I opened my glove compartment and took out the two-inch dowels I kept in there for good luck. They also made it a lot easier to get into the joint that had a metal detector. With your fist wrapped around the links of wood, they also made it vastly easier to break a guy's jaw. I got out of the car and opened the trunk. I handed Eddie's guy one of the batons I'd found so useful taking on the street gangs around Central Terminal. After Lexi had lent one to me I knew I had to have a couple of these beauties. They were about the size of a folded-up umbrella but could instantly be snapped open to about two feet of stainless steel that was death on shin bones, arm bones, and collar bones. I showed the guy how to snap it to full length with just the flick of his wrist.

"Wow," he said. "This thing is so light. Thanks, man."

I tossed another one to his buddy. "These aren't for keeps, gentlemen. I expect them back when our adventure is over. They don't have to be in pristine condition when I get them back, though. In fact, I'm hoping they aren't."

Both guys snapped the batons open a few times and I could see they had the hang of it. Eddie had an old panel truck we would use to get to the Loading Dock, and if all went well, back home. We were about to move when I told the newbies how much I appreciated their participation. I knew Murman knew how much I appreciated him.

"I'm sure Eddie told you the goons would be strapped. I don't know if you guys are but I'm not. If you see a gun those batons will significantly impair the shooter's gun hand, if you get my drift. Don't fuck around. Smack the shit out of the gun hand as quick as you can. Don't be shy. No one is calling fouls in this game. The winners go home and the losers go to the hospital. Got it?"

They nodded and one of the guys lifted his sweatshirt to show me he was carrying. I didn't need to ask Eddie. I pulled an Armored Republic vest out of the truck and strapped it on and pulled my lucky St. Bonaventure jacket over it. Then we got in the truck and headed for the target. I briefed the guys as we rode.

"Simple is best," I said. "I'll go in the front door and start asking around about the missing girl. That's what the kid did before he got the shit beat out of him. The goons hustled him out the back door and that's where the beating took place. I'm betting they try the same shit with me but when we come out the back, I won't be alone. Pick a guy and disable him. Be quick too. I don't want to take too bad a beating while you guys get in the game, capisce?"

Both guys nodded and we rode the rest of the way in silence. We got to the place just before eleven. I got out of the truck about a block away from the front door and put the dowels into my pants pockets and the girl's picture in my shirt pocket. Eddie and the bruisers would find a good spot for the truck and get in position near the back door of the club. I walked to the front door wishing I had a sap or a baton or something that would help me defend myself but if this joint had a metal detector that whole plan would go to shit. I got that pre-"game" lump in the pit of my stomach as I reached the door. I didn't wait to be challenged by the bouncer at the door.

"HEY, HULK, I NEED SOME HELP." I was yelling to be heard over the noise inside, but I needn't have bothered. The guy gave me blank stare but opened the swinging doors to let me in. The noise was a few dozen decibels above deafening and the strobe lights added to the frenzied state of play. There were a hundred or so people on the dance floor but damned if I could tell who was with whom. As I made my way toward the long bar that ran across the back wall, I noticed more than a few dancers with that glazed-over look in their eyes. It was the kind of look that comes from something a lot more potent than booze, a look I'd seen a lot of during my employ in Cabo San Jose. There was some bad shit going on in here; I could feel it crawling all over my skim. I reached the bar and got the attention of the barmaid version of the illustrated man. She came over but didn't smile until I complimented her.

"Great ink!" I lied, when, in fact, she looked like an infant had scribbled on her arms with Sharpies.

"Thanks, dude. They're about half done. My guy has to do the color infill in a few weeks."

Now that I had her attention, I pulled Jennifer Norton's picture from my pocket.

"This girl is missing and I'm helping her parents try to find her. She look familiar?"

"You a cop, dude?"

"No, I'm not. I'm just trying to help some worried parents. Seen her around?"

"Put that damn thing away, Dude, before the muscle here sees you. It ain't healthy asking questions in here." Her eyes darted around the room faster than the flashing strobes.

"Just tell me if you've seen the girl and I'll be out of here in a flash."

I saw the terror in the girl's eyes before I felt the big hand smack me in the back.

"Hey asshole, you're keeping the bartender from her job. Time for you to leave." He had me by the back of my shirt and yanked me roughly from the bar. I didn't want to run the risk of giving my play away too early so I took a step toward the door I'd entered. I didn't get very far.

"Oh no, asshole," he said, pulling me in another direction, "we have a special door for scumbags like you." Another guy appeared on my left and the two thugs virtually swept me off my feet and headed me toward a door at the far end of the long bar. Two giants just about carrying a guy out was either a pretty common occurrence or the clientele was too far gone to notice or care. I was struggling to get my hands free enough to get them around the dowels but the grip of these two thugs felt like steel bands on my arms. But the situation resolved itself when we shuffled through the backroom and I was thrown out the door. I thought the tough guys might deprive me of retribution by heading back inside but thankfully, they weren't done with me yet ... nor I with them. They came down the stairs just as I fitted my fists around the dowels, but my ersatz brass knuckles couldn't save me from a hard kick in the ribs. I rolled away from the kick, struggling to refill my lungs. The familiar sound of steel on skull encouraged me to stand. One of Murray's guys had clubbed one of the thugs to his knees. Murray used a sap to fell the other guy. I figured Eddie and our other friend had that situation in hand so I went to the bouncer on his knees and bleeding from the scalp. I lined up a right cross that landed just below his ear. The crunch from his jaw gave me confidence that this piece of shit would be sipping his meals through a straw for a couple of months.

"About that door reserved for scumbags like me," I said, lifting his head up by the hair, "you're going to be wishing we went out the front door in a minute."

Eddie's guy kicked him in the gut, and he fell on his face. Murray and his guy had turned the other thug's face into hamburger. I walked over to him and whispered in his ear.

"Never fuck with a GI, asshole. There's too many of us." With that, I punched him hard in the throat. He rolled over into the dirt, his blood turning it to mud. Eddie looked at me and we silently agreed our work here was done, at least for now. We still had the matter of Jennifer Norton to resolve but that was for another day. We gathered up our stuff and I followed Murray to the truck. Along the way, I realized my ribs took way more of the kick than I'd realized. My breathing was raspy, and each breath hurt like I was getting kicked all over again. Murman must have noticed because he stuck his shoulder under mine and helped me make it to the truck. As we drove to South Buffalo, we did an impromptu after action-report. I was the only friendly casualty and that was the way it should be. The bait always ran that risk. I knew we did OK when Murray offered that we should have killed those guys. Maybe, I thought, but there is still time, and I knew this wasn't over by a long shot yet.

CHAPTER FIFTEEN

After doling out my thanks to Eddie's bouncers and to Ed himself and collecting the toys I'd allowed the bouncers to play with, I got into the Audi struggling to keep the guys from seeing how much pain I was in. With the adrenalin rush from the fight gone, my ribs throbbed with every breath. It was late but I called Lexi anyway, knowing she'd be pissed she wasn't included in our boys' night out. Better to deal with that now, I reasoned, but the call went to voice mail. I felt around my left side to get an idea if the ribs were broken. Going to the emergency room was a non-starter. All I would get there would be a couple hours long wait for an x-ray and the advice to take some ibuprofen. It was after two a.m. when I pulled into West Ferry. When I did, I saw Lexi's Jeep. I was not in the mood for a heavy-duty confrontation tonight but I was glad to see she was here. When I opened my door, she was pacing a path through my rug.

"Where the hell have you been?" she said, in a voice too loud for this late hour. "I've been calling you for the past two hours."

I related the events of the evening as dispassionately as possible. It would have made Lexi even madder if I sounded like I enjoyed it.

"Sonofabitch! You went without me!" That got me a punch on the arm that caused my beat-up ribs to hurt. I tried to avoid letting her know I'd been hurt but she saw me wince.

"What? You got hurt? Goddamn you, Coe Duffy. You went out to play and left me home. See what happens when I'm not around to protect you?" I expected another whack but was surprised by a gentle kiss. Lexi got close enough to lift my shirt and winced a little herself when she saw my bruised ribs.

"I don't suppose you had those looked at," she said. I proceeded to tell her why I hadn't.

"I hate to admit this, but you're probably right." She talked over her shoulder as she went to the refrigerator for ice. A girlfriend who knows about pain is often an advantage. I made my way to the couch and laid back to rest or a minute. Lexi had the ice in a zip lock bag and wrapped it with a dishtowel. She put it gently on my side and knelt next to the couch and spoke softly to me.

"Now give me all the gory details about kicking the shit out of those assholes and I might forgive you for not including me."

I remember starting in with the narrative but awoke with a bag of water on the floor next to me. The sounds coming from the kitchen gave me hope that I might have achieved an emotional breakthrough with Lexi having spent the night so it was all I could do to hide my disappointment when half-sister Sheila emerged from the kitchen with coffee and a new ice bag.

"Good morning, my un-caped crusader. Still can't seem to leave well enough alone, I see."

"If you mean was I going to sit back and let a good kid get his ass kicked for trying to find his lost sister, then hell no, I can't leave that alone." She was smiling when she handed me the coffee.

"So it's just a matter of phrasing, I suppose," she said, placing the ice over my black-and-blue ribs.

"What are you doing here?" I said. "Don't you have history to preserve?"

"I like to balance my dedication to history with a commitment to the present," she said. "Your friend Lexi called mother last night after you fell asleep. She asked me to drop in to see if you were okay."

"You may report back that I'm sore but intact," I said.

"You may render that report to mother in your own voice," Sheila said.

"She had an early appointment but said she'd be stopping in afterwards. You must know, Coe, she's not pleased. She thinks you have inherited a death wish from your father and are in frantic pursuit of realizing it."

"That's ridiculous! Death wish … how absurd …"

"Is it? Is it really? Look around you. You have achieved a comfortable life here with a caring, if unconventional, family, a beautiful and accomplished girlfriend, and means to continue to live this life. Yet you go to Mexico to involve yourself in ugly business of no concern to you. You risk life and limb in some pursuit better left to the police. Why don't you let well-enough alone and enjoy life?"

I started to respond but Sheila raised her hand to stop me.

"I was the warm-up act for mother. Save your answers for her. But know this; we are very concerned about you, Coe, and we see the continuing turmoil that swirls around you as a troubling pattern."

With that, Sheila bent and kissed my cheek and gave me a wave.

"History needs me now." With that she was gone, leaving me with that intoxicating scent of her perfume, my coffee, and some aching ribs. I knew another ache was on the way when my mother arrived, and I wasn't sure if she wouldn't be worse than bruised ribs. It didn't take long to find out. I was letting the tea steep in advance of Marsha's arrival, but I needn't have bothered. She was hot enough to brew the tea with the heat of her anger. She entered without a knock.

"What will it take, Coe?"

My look must have told her I didn't know what she meant.

"What will it take for you to get over the notion you are indestructible, that you can will your way through any situation? How many broken bones, how many stitches, how many concussions will it take to make you realize that what's driving you is nothing more than a demented death wish?"

She paused to take a breath and I seized the moment.

"Marsha, please sit down. I think you are overreacting. I'm just trying help a guy find his sister. Don't be so melodramatic." Her silence told me unmistakably that I'd screwed up. She sat at end of the couch, quietly composing herself.

"Helping that poor boy would have been actually finding his sister," she said. "Helping him was getting him into the hospital where he could be properly cared for. Helping him was calling your friend at the Defense Department to spare the boy more trouble.

"But that wasn't good enough for you. You couldn't help in any real way. You had to avenge the boy. You had to put yourself in harm's way once more. You had to test yourself once more by proving how brave and tough you are. You wade into danger with both feet, with fists flying, with danger all around you so you can emerge once more as Coe the conquering hero."

She paused again but I had no witty retort. She was telling a morbid, painful truth about me. I could handle the morbid but the truth of it all was the pain – a pain worse than that in my side. I wondered if I really was that psychologically damaged that I kept demanding so much of myself.

"You're right, Marsha. I didn't do a damned thing for that kid by going to the Loading Dock. I didn't do it for him. I did it for me. Those thugs hurt Norton so I wanted, I needed, to hurt them."

Marsha was calmer now. She went to the kitchen and poured herself some tea, then moved closer to me on the couch and took my hand.

"You are in way over your head," she said. "My sources tell me the night club is owned by a Russian. The thugs you beat up are not local. God knows where they are from. What's clear is that these are not the same street toughs you dealt with at Central Terminal. This is a whole other kind of nasty. That's why you must let the authorities deal with them. You don't have the resources to make this your fight."

It is never easy to hear that kind of advice. It is even harder to hear it from one's mother. But the worst of it was my mother was right. We'd won a skirmish, but we might have started something on a larger, more dangerous level.

Marsha smiled at me.

"Your wonderful friend Lexi has assured me she would do her best to bring the police department to bear on this situation. She cares deeply for you, you know."

I smiled back.

"You have my word, Marsha. I'm standing down. We'll let the big boys handle to situation now."

"Seriously? How can I believe you since you promised me at the hospital that you wouldn't do anything stupid?"

"Well, I didn't do anything stupid. Mother. It was all a well-executed plan."

I got a hint of a smile from her with that, and I moved closer to her.

"I promise. No more smart or stupid shit. I'm serious as a heart attack."

Marsha finished her tea and rose from the couch.

"You need to work on your metaphors and remember your promise to me." I walked her to the door and kissed her cheek. "I promise," I repeated. I filled the zip lock bag with fresh ice and lay back down on the couch to ice my aching ribs. I was weaving in and out of sleep when my phone snapped me out of my drifting. When I saw that it was Lexi calling, I began steeling myself for more verbal abuse.

"Hey ..." that was as far as she let me get.

"Shut up and listen! The cops found Jennifer Norton. She was in a stupor at the train station downtown. They've taken her to ECMC and think she was drugged. I'm going to wait for word from them. She was in pretty rough shape according to Denise Crawford."

"Come and get me and I'll wait with you."

"No chance of that. I'm almost there and I am not coming back for you. Take care of those ribs and I'll let you know when I learn something." With that, she ended the call and I was left with lots of questions, few answers and my improvised ice bag leaking on my rug. I grabbed a dishtowel from the kitchen and dumped the melting ice into the sink. I went out on my terrace to take in some sun and warm air. I tried to figure out how Jennifer had wound up alone at the depot. I didn't think she could escape in the condition they found her, so what had happened? Could her captors just have dumped her? Why would they if they thought she could tell the cops what happened to her? Just what the hell was going on? I was looking out over the city from the terrace, taking note of all the steeples that rose up over the trees and houses. For a city with this many churches, there was something fetid and evil going on. But how evil? I needed answers but all I had swirling around in my head were questions and I had to rely on my pissed off girl friend to provide some of those answers. I thought about driving myself over to the hospital to wait with Lexi but that thought passed quickly when I turned to go back into my apartment and a bolt of pain shot up my side. I guess, weighing the alternatives, waiting wasn't so bad after all. I loaded up my bag with ice and went back to the couch. I must have dozed off for when I opened my eyes, Lexi was sitting across from me drinking one of my Stella Artois' from the bottle. I might have asked how she got in but given my doorman's affinity for her I figured I knew the answer already.

"Good thing you woke up," she said. "I was about to wake you and I don't think you would have liked that." She was still mad, damn.

"How's the girl?" I asked.

"She's not good. The docs told my cop friends she was lucky to be alive with the big dose of smack she got hit with. The ambulance crew that picked her up hit her with a couple sprays of Narcan and that's the difference between us hoping for her recovery and mourning her death. She's barely awake and is going through some mental trauma that sends her into a frenzy periodically."

"Did you notify her parents?"

"Yeah, the cops did that. I saw the Norton come through the waiting area while I was still waiting for news."

"Well, their twins might be a little worse for wear but at least they are still alive," I said.

"Not so fast with the rosy outlook. The girl is not out of the woods yet. The docs warned Denise that it would be a while before they could question her and that she might have some psychological issues from the drugs. They know she took a big hit of heroin, but they were checking for other substances. Remember we found that partially dissolved tab of Ambien. If she has a lot of that in her system, it could be long-term trouble. A lot of bad shit happens when you take a lot of that stuff.

"Speaking of bad shit, how are you feeling?"

"I'm coming along," I said. "I'm thinking about going out to walk a little. I don't think I'm ready to run yet and the gym is a week or so off. Feel like going for a walk with me?"

"Hell no. I'm going to see if I can get a lead on what has happened to the Nortons. Finding the girl has pissed a lot of my friends in the department off. I do what I can to help them." She was heading toward the door and I called after her.

"Be careful. Lexi. I think we're dealing with some bad actors."

She stopped to give me one of her patented glares.

"No shit, Sherlock. Just heal quickly. We might have some work to do."

With Lexi gone, I suited up for a little walk around the block. My ribs were pretty sore but I knew I could tolerate the pain. I'd dealt with worse. I walked out to West Ferry and felt the bracing slap of the still chilly air on my face. Spring was close but not here yet. I headed west toward Elmwood Avenue figuring that distance would be a good start for now. The trees were trying to go green despite the chill and I knew it wouldn't be long before the leaves would be out in all their green brilliance. I made it to Elmwood without too much discomfort and I thought I'd stretch the walk out a little. I headed north and figured I could make it around the long block back to Delaware. I probably shouldn't have.

While I turned the corner on Cleveland to head east, I was being tracked by an unlikely and unseen pair of eyes. Dora, who had set all this in motion, was perched on a stool at Spot Coffee. As soon as she saw me, she was on her cell phone.

"Yeah, I'm watching him now," she said. "He's heading down Cleveland toward Delaware. Hell yeah, I'm sure it's him. Follow him, my ass. He wasn't real happy with me the last time I talked to him. Alright, alright … don't get your pubes on fire. I'm on him."

As I made my way back home, I was unaware of the attention I'd attracted. It used to be said what you don't know can't hurt you. Don't believe it.

CHAPTER SIXTEEN

W HILE I RE-ICED MY ribs, Lexi sat with half a dozen current and former cops, all women of course. They might have all been women, but they were all to be taken seriously. Among them, they had nine citations for bravery above and beyond the call. They had eleven medals in various hues ranging from Gold to Bronze. One of them was a renowned bodybuilder and two others were martial arts experts. In short, these cops were officers to be reckoned with. They sat at a round table at the Bijou eating and drinking on my tab.

Detective Redmond was leading a discussion about the problem of the Loading Dock. She scrupulously took notes about what they knew, how much they surmised, and what was the best way to fill in the blanks. Lexi was the only one of her posse that had been to the place even though she hadn't actually been inside.

"The place is a shithole," Lexi said. "They have to be violating a hundred or so building codes. I wonder how they haven't gotten on the Liquor Authority's radar. But what grabs me is the fact that someone is drugging people in the place. No one takes Ambien to get a buzz."

Lindsay said that my experience smacked of "some nefarious shit."

"Not one legitimate joint has bouncers pull that kind of shit," she said. "It doesn't matter that Coe and company kicked some serious ass. Something is very wrong about that joint."

"Let's not get too far off the topic of what happened to the twins." Denise

Crawford was speaking and that made the others listen intently. She had retired from the force but not before running up a record that most male officers could only hope to match.

"We have a guy beaten senseless a week before we find the sister he was searching for thrown away like trash. Stay on that topic. Any thoughts why they would get rid of the girl that way?"

"I'm thinking the brother and then Coe looking for the girl made the honchos think she was bringing too much heat, so she was disposable," Lexi said.

"But why let her live?" Cat said. "Why not just kill her?"

"I think they tried to," Lindsay said. "They thought they'd given her a big enough dose to kill her. They didn't count on her being found in time to save her."

"Do we know how the Norton girl wound up at the train station?' Crawford asked.

"There has to be a camera or two in the area," Redmond said. "I'll check into that. Should I have some squad cars make some extra circuits around the place?"

"I would hold off on that," Crawford said. "These guys are already scared. That's why they dumped the girl. Let's make them think the pressure is off and see if they do something else stupid."

With that, they rose and agreed to meet again the next day – at my place. Lexi called to catch me up and to tell me she'd volunteered my place for the next meeting. It wasn't a big deal as I had easily enough room and enough refreshments, but Lexi made me rethink that.

"Lindsay is an enthusiastic beer drinker and Cat can drink her body weight in merlot, so you better stock up."

"Do you want me to order and you pick up or just have it delivered?"

"Is that your sly way of asking me to come over tonight?"

I hadn't thought it very sly, but I played along.

"Well, yeah. You know I always love to see you. So you can pick the stuff up?"

"Yeah, but I ain't schlepping it up to your place."

"Not a problem. Just wink at Simon and he'll carry the beer, the wine, the snacks, and you up here." That got a laugh out of her and that put a smile on my face. She said she'd stop by the stores and see me in a couple of hours. I knew she'd be hungry, so I also ordered delivery from LaNova Pizza. My ribs didn't hurt nearly as much as they did when Lexi was mad at me.

As I headed into the shower, Dora was noting my location.

"He lives in some big-assed apartment building right near Delaware," she said into the phone. "Am I through now?" Her mission completed, she headed back to the Elmwood strip.

•••

An hour or so later, Simon buzzed me on the intercom.

"Coe, it's Simon, your friendly doorman." I guess it was lost on him that no one else could access the intercom system. You have a delivery from LaNova."

"Can you bring it up for me, Simon? I'm still healing from some badly bruised ribs."

A minute later, Simon had an armful of pizza, chicken wings, and antipasto. I told him to put it on the kitchen counter and gave him a tip larger than he deserved.

"Lexi is coming by in a bit and she has a bunch of beer and wine for a gathering I'm having tomorrow. Could you carry it up for her?"

"Sure thing, boss. I'd do it just to ride on the elevator with her and dig her perfume." He was going to continue until I snatched the tip back from him.

"Lust in silence, Simon, especially when talking about Lexi."

"Right," he said. "Sometimes I say the thought part out loud. No offense, boss."

"None taken," I said, handing him back the tip.

The pizza was still hot when Lexi showed up.

"LaNova? How did you know I'd be famished?" Have I mentioned that

Lexi was the only person I know that could tell the origin of pizza just by its smell? In a city like Buffalo with its infinite variety of great pizza, that was a talent.

"You are always hungry," I said, earning a punch on the arm.

Simon entered behind her with the beer and wine.

"Damn, boss, you having a party tomorrow or what?"

"Just a few friends, Simon. Nothing special."

"And his friends are all women, Simon," Lexi said. "Wait till you see them."

With that, I gave the doorman another generous tip and ushered him to the door.

"You shouldn't tease him, Lexi, He's horny enough already." She responded by heading into the kitchen and filling a plate with pizza and wings.

"There is something pleasantly decadent about eating chicken wings off a Wedgewood plate," she said.

"Please don't make a big deal of that tomorrow night" I said, filling my own plate. "You know Marsha had this place furnished when I moved in. I would have been okay with paper plates."

"Coe Duffy, how many times must I tell you? I love showing you off."

I opened a couple of beers, and we enjoyed our repast in silence. When we finished, we moved to my sofa and Lexi gave me a rundown on what her pals talked about over at the Bijou. We were both intrigued by the release of the Norton girl. Lexi repeated her theory that the girl was causing too much trouble for them, and they decided they didn't need the aggravation. Then she added her pals were checking for security cameras near the train station to determine how she got there.

"By the way," Lexi said, "we put our drinks on your tab." I let that slide.

"That's a great approach," I said. "The Loading Dock isn't too far away but in the condition Jennifer Norton was in it might as well have been ten miles. Figuring out how she got there would be a big help. Those gorillas from the Dock couldn't have been dumb enough to take her there themselves."

Lexi nestled into my good side and we sat in silence for a few minutes.

Then I asked Lexi about the team she had assembled. I was suitably impressed when she told me.

"Damn, that's the distaff all-star team," I said.

"Distaff, my ass," she said. "I'd put those women up against anyone in the department, male or female."

"Easy, champ" I said, stroking her hair and kissing her forehead. "I've seen you in action and if they are half as good as you, you got some kick-ass team."

Her team included Cat Redmond who I knew, and Lindsay Zgoda who I knew about, Denise Crawford who every cop in Buffalo knew, Lexi said she had a couple more women in mind but didn't tell me who they might be. That calmed her down, so much so, in fact, she fell asleep with her head in my lap. But her sleep didn't last long. Her cell phone buzzed, and she was awake.

"Yeah," she answered. "Whoa, that's awesome. Were you able to see the plate? Great … let me know when you learn more."

"Damn, Coe, I think we caught a big break," she said.

"Don't tell me … there was a camera near the depot, and it picked up someone dropping the Norton girl off."

That got me a punch on the arm.

"Yeah, how did you know?"

I told her I could tell just from her end of the conversation but that didn't slow her down.

"It was a cab that dropped her off," she said. "All we need is the cab number or the plate and we can figure out who hired the cab; another step closer."

That scenario didn't seem right to me.

"Wait, so you think these goons shot our gal up almost to the point of death then called a cab for her? That doesn't make any sense."

Lexi stood and started pacing. Two laps of my living room and she sat down again.

"You're right. That doesn't fly. Maybe we'll figure it out after Cat tracks down the cabbie."

We sat on the sofa for a bit but I knew she was getting ready to leave. When she is on a mission, she focuses like a laser beam. That's what made her such a great cop. Rather than make her feel guilty about bailing, I stood up and went to my freezer to refill my ice bag.

"Lexi, I'm going to take a pain pill and ice these battered ribs some more so I'll probably be nodding off. You can stay if you like but I am not going to be very good company."

"Who said you are good company without the pain pill?" she laughed and stood.

"I'm going to go home and see if I can put together what we know in some reasonable narrative. I told the girls to be here for lunch tomorrow. That's OK, right?"

"Sure. Will the antipastos be enough or do you have carnivores in the group as well?"

She assured me there would be enough to munch on while they were thinking. Then she gave me a big wet kiss with her fingers kneading the back of my head. She always did that when she was going out of reach, damn her. I got my ice, swallowed my pill dry and went back to the couch to settle in. Before I dozed off, I was visited by some notion of the horrors Jennifer Norton must have endured before being found. I came to a few hours later, just lucid enough to get myself into bed.

•••

I woke up feeling pretty good. The pain in my ribs had subsided to a dull ache so I decided I might try a little run before Lexi and her friends arrived. I went on to the terrace to gauge the temperature. It was one of those perfect early spring mornings with the warmth winning its tug-of-war with the lingering winter chill. I got into my running clothes, downed a few ibuprofen, and headed to the elevator. Simon was surprised to see me.

"Hey Coe, you feeling OK?"

"I'll tell you when I get back. The ribs are feeling pretty good, though. I'm going to start out small and make the circuit down to Elmwood, up to Cleveland, and back on Delaware. If I am not back in fifteen minutes or so, let Marsha know."

"Will do, boss. Go easy on yourself."

I hit West Ferry in a light jog and felt pretty good. The morning air was perfect, and I picked up the pace a little as I made the turn at Elmwood. It was early so the sidewalks were pretty empty and not like the obstacle course the pedestrians would make them by noon, so I accelerated a little more. The sweat was starting to bead on my forehead by the time I hit Cleveland Avenue and I picked up the pace again. Unbeknownst to me, my jog was being reported as I ran down Cleveland.

"Yeah, it's him," Dora said, perched on a stool in the window of Spot Coffee. "He's running up Cleveland. No! Nobody's chasing him! He's running, like for exercise. Yeah, yeah, yeah … I'll keep an eye on him."

By the time I hit Delaware, I was feeling like my old self, but I eased off the tempo even so. No sense in hurting anything, I reasoned, but planned on hitting the cemetery run tomorrow. I got back to the condo much quicker than I'd anticipated. Even Simon noticed.

"Hey Coe, did you catch a cab or something?"

I let that one slide.

"I'm having some guests for lunch, Simon: Lexi and some of her friends."

"That should be interesting."

"Too much interest just might get your ass kicked, buddy. These are some of the toughest chicks you've ever laid eyes on and if I were you, that's all I'd lay on them."

Simon was grinning that insipid grin for which he was semi-famous, but I knew he was taking what I'd said seriously, as well he should.

I hustled up to my condo and jumped in the shower to get ready for the gathering. This was going to be an interesting day.

I'd just finished putting out glasses and small plates when Lexi arrived.

"I thought I'd come a little early to help you set up but I'm too late, huh?"

"What's to set up?" I said. "This took all of five minutes."

"How are you feeling? Are you up to host us?"

I laughed and said I was fine.

"Besides, it's a little late to ask, isn't it?"

That earned me a punch on the arm but not a serious one. I told her about my jaunt around the block and how good I felt running. For some reason, that earned me a hug. I resolved one day to figure out Lexi's system of rewards and punishments but that could wait. I shined up the glasses while Lexi rearranged the plates I'd set out just because she could. It didn't take long for the ladies to arrive. Simon gave me a buzz and announced their arrival. Two minutes later, Lexi was showing them around my condo, pointing out various features my mother thought appropriate for her only son.

"Damn, Coe, this is some sweet place," Denise Crawford said, a sentiment repeated by the others. I showed them a few of the things Lexi had overlooked like my bidet in the master bathroom. That was a big hit until I told them I'd never used the spray and dry feature.

"Oh hell, Coe, live a little," Cat Redmond said. "Everyone deserves a spritz now and then."

"You are welcome to be the inaugural user of that feature if you like," I said.

"Bullshit," Lexi said. "If anyone breaks the thing in it's going to be me."

They got down to business after I took the women out on the terrace and impressed them with my view.

"Coe, you are the only one who has actually been inside the place," Lindsay said. "What should we know about it?"

The question got me to wondering what the gals had in mind, but I held off asking.

"Nothing remarkable about the place except the security," I said. "There were five on duty the night I went: the doorman, two bouncers, and two bartenders, one of them a woman. The guys looked like they shopped at 'Hulks Are Us.'"

"But we hit them on an off night so there could be more goons on week-ends. The clientele was typical; young people on the dance floor, some paired off in booths along the walls. It's very dark with most of the light coming from the bar area. There is a door left of the bar that opens to the back of the place. That's the door they threw me out of."

For some reason, that drew a few chuckles from the women.

"Why the need for this information? You aren't planning on doing something silly are you?" I asked. I thought it best to change the subject.

"What about catching that cab on the surveillance camera? Did that lead go anywhere?"

Cat told us the cops tracked down the driver who admitted leaving the Norton girl at the train depot.

"But he said he found the girl laying on the side of Exchange Street," she said. "He didn't want to leave her on the street, so he put her in the cab. He said he started carrying Nar-Can after a fare OD-ed in his cab. He gave her a squirt and dropped her at the depot. He said he figured someone would come along and take care of her. According to the cabbie, the girl was never lucid enough to speak and he didn't know what else to do with her."

"That cabbie might have saved her life. Has anyone checked on her to-day?" I asked. "Is she coming out of the stupor?"

Denise said she had called the hospital, but the girl was still out of it.

I made a promise to my mother that I kept squarely in mind when I offered a solution that wouldn't be a solution.

"Well, we got the GI back and his sister and that's what we started out to do," I said. "We could just declare ourselves the winners and walk off the field."

"Bullshit!" Lexi said. "We got the twins back in a lot worse shape than we bargained for. Someone is going to pay for that. Coe, didn't you talk to the bar backs when you went to the Loading Dock with Eddie Murray? Did you learn anything that might be useful?"

"Well, two guys were smoking dope behind the place when Eddie and I rolled up. They were pretty wasted but one of the guys said a white van would pull up some nights and a bunch of girls would be ushered into the club but he didn't know where the van came from or who the girls were."

That started some conversations among the team that I couldn't hear. I think Lexi wanted it that way, so I headed to the kitchen to mix the antipasto and warm the chicken wings, I put some Cokes, wine, water, and salad dressings on the bar and announced that the women could eat. They ended their confab and came out to the kitchen.

"Really Coe," Denise said, "Wedgewood plates?"

I was about to respond when Lexi interrupted with the story about how my mother had furnished and outfitted the place before I moved in.

"You don't really think a guy like Coe would have asked for a bidet, do you?"

For some reason that got a big laugh.

We talked while we ate, and the consensus was that Cat would take what we'd discovered back to police headquarters and let them do an official visit to the Loading Dock to see if they could uncover any violations or criminal activity. I was in complete agreement,

"You gals would just be stirring the pot with more trouble," I said. "Let the cops do the heavy work."

That comment wasn't well-received by the group, but even with the combined skills of their group, the job was best left to the police.

"There's some nasty stuff going on in that dive and other stuff even nastier that we have no clue about," Lexi said. "Let's hope a raid will bring some real heat on the place."

With that, Lexi and crew cleaned up the plates and took care of the leftovers. The women headed for the door. Lexi stayed behind with me.

"What are you up to this afternoon?" she said.

"I might go to the gym," I said. "My little run yesterday felt okay but I don't want to push it."

Lexi headed toward the door but stopped.

"By the way, I left you voice mail about a sighting of the grubby kid who got you started on the trail of the Nortons. Did you hear it yet?"

"No, too much crap going on. Where did you see her?"

"Lindsay and I spotted her up on Elmwood handing out flyers for the

Loading Dock."

I started to say something but thought better of it, and let Lexi leave with her friends. But as I sat on the couch, the Dora sighting was a direct connection between her and the Loading Dock. I had assumed that connection previously, but Lexi's tidbit was proof positive. I thought about doing a search for the girl on my own to see what new information she might be able to provide, but thought better of it. Even with the improvement in the condition of my ribs, I was still less than a hundred percent physically. I also thought confronting her might scare her off before I could get any significant information out of her. I stuck to my plan, threw on my gym clothes, and headed to KC's to sweat out some frustration.

•••

At police headquarters, Cat Redmond was working up a sweat but nowhere near as productively as I was. She was trying to impress upon her bosses the need for an incursion into the Loading Dock.

"Jeez, Cat, you want us to barge into the place on that thin thread of so-called evidence of yours? We'll never get a judge to sign a warrant for us on that."

Redmond was hardly surprised at Captain Dale's reluctance to push the case. He'd risen through the ranks of the department with an almost pathological aversion to conflict. He never questioned an order, never pursued a shaky case, and never really distinguished himself in any way as a cop except for his exceptional level of mediocrity. But he had finally risen to his level of incompetency as head of narcotics. Dale didn't like to make waves. Waves scared him because he couldn't swim against the departmental headwinds.

"I'll have the cars on patrol swing by there for a couple of nights, Cat. That's the best you can do."

"No," Cat said, "that's not the best you can do, Captain. It's the only thing you'll do."

She went back to her desk to convey the bad news to her posse.

CHAPTER SEVENTEEN

SHAUGHNESSY'S WAS ON THE way back from the gym so I decided to hydrate at Eddie's place. When I walked in, I gave some approving nods to the bartenders and bouncers who'd made the incursion into the Loading Dock. I figured they had a lot to smile about as they didn't get their ribs pulverized.

"Hello lads," I said. "Is the proprietor around?"

"He's on his way back from a doctor appointment," one of the guys said. "Have a cold one on him." With that, he snapped the cap of a frosty Budweiser and put it in front of me.

"You must have read my mind. The only thing better than a cold beer after a workout is a free one." I was on my second one when Mur-man came through the door. I could sense a slap on the back coming so I turned a little on the stool to let him hit the good side.

"How are you doing, kid?" he said, taking the stool next to me. I gave him the Reader's Digest version of my ribs and filled him in on the developments in the Jennifer Norton episode.

"Fucking animals," he said and motioned to the barman for a beer. "Why do you figure they let her go?"

"They probably figured she was getting to be more of a problem than an asset, what with her brother coming around and then our little venture."

"But they let her live?"

"I don't think they meant to. She had an awful lot of smack in her system. They probably thought it would kill her when they dumped her in the gutter like garbage. The cabbie probably saved her with a shot of Nar-Can. Hell, she still hasn't been lucid enough to talk."

"That's where we're at now? Cabbies carrying Nar-Can? The assholes need to be taught a much bigger lesson," Eddie said. I could just about see the steam coming out of his ears.

I filled him in on the chat I'd had with Lexi and company.

"I think the cops might be taking over the lead," I said.

"The law is too good for them. They need to be treated like they treated these girls. They need a real ass-kicking."

"Maybe," I said, "but I'm taking a bit of a sabbatical from ass-kicking for the time being." Eddie laughed and clicked his bottle off mine.

"You know your old man would be proud as hell at what you're doing," he said.

I laughed.

"What am I doing, Ed? I made a score at the Terminal and have been shittin' in high cotton ever since."

"Hey, you can't bullshit the bull," he laughed. "I know how you've been helping out schools and charities and the like. I also know if it weren't for you, that girl would have still been abused by those slobs at the Loading Dock. You are doing some good stuff, kid."

We clinked bottles again. In fact, we clinked a bottle or two more than I should have. I had a long drive back to my condo and though I knew a lot of Buffalo cops, I didn't want to push my luck. When I stood to leave, I didn't move fast enough to keep Eddie from hugging me. I suppressed a shout when my sore ribs protested and let it out after I got in my car. The drive back north was going smoothly, until Lexi called.

"Cat just told me her bosses are less than impressed with what she presented to them," she said. "So they wouldn't agree to anything more than to run a few patrols cars by the place from time to time. That was the worst part about being a cop – dealing with the bosses who weren't smart enough to get out of their own way."

"Calm down, Lexi. You and I both knew what we had didn't amount to a lot, not in terms of evidence, anyway. Departments are running scared these days about civil rights and stuff. We take what we can get and move on."

I changed the subject to something more pleasant.

"I'm on my way back from Eddie's place. Do you want to do something for dinner?"

"I don't know. I'm too pissed off to think about that right now. I'll call you in a bit."

With that, she was gone. I knew she was angry, but I didn't know how angry until she said she was too mad to think about dinner. I was almost home when I got another call from one of the women in my life.

"Coe, do you have a few minutes to talk?" It was Sheila for whom I also had a few minutes to listen, which is what she really meant.

"Sure. Want to meet me at Cole's?"

"I'd rather you come by my office. I'll wait for you. Just ring the bell and Vera will let you in."

"I'll be there in ten minutes," I said, but I made it in five.

Vera, doorkeeper at the Historical Society, answered promptly when I rang. She had on her usual "just sucked on a lemon face".

"Hello, Beautiful, working late?"

Her face puckered even more.

"I trust your business with Miss Sheila won't take too long," she said. "I'd like to be home at a reasonable hour."

"I'm here at her request, Vera. As soon as she's finished, we're finished."

She closed and locked the door behind me while I went down the stairs to Sheila's office. It was well past her normal quitting time, and she looked like she was sitting for a photo shoot for Vogue. She came from behind the desk and started to hug me, but I'd already met my hugging quota for the day. My ribs wouldn't take another. So she kissed my cheeks instead and sat next to me.

"Do you know a woman named Colleen Mayer?" she asked.

"Doesn't sound familiar," I said.

"She is an investigator with a federal agency; with HUD specifically."

"Yeah, she's Lexi's friend. Lexi got all energized because the Mayer woman took her on a stakeout. It had something to do with cleaning crews doing a hell of a lot more than cleaning houses. Damn, how do you know her?"

"Buffalo is a small town, Coe. You know that. Everyone knows everyone."

Sheila went on to relate a conversation she'd had with Mayer at a fundraiser for the Burchfield-Penny Art Gallery. Mayer had given photographic evidence of the cleaning crews ransacking several houses to the FBI along with details of her tailing their vans. The agents got warrants and raided the warehouse where the ill-gotten gains were stored.

"Great," I said. "Another win for the good guys."

"I'm not finished, Coe. While the agents were searching the building, they came across some smaller rooms off the main room. In those rooms, they found women's clothing and a bunch of slingers advertising the Loading Dock night club."

"Holy shit. That's a connection between the dirtbags emptying the houses and the scumbags running that shithole that passes for a night club."

"It would appear that, although you have different pejoratives for each, the people running both enterprises are one and the same."

"This is good news," I said. Then, I went on to sketch out some of the discussions I'd had with Lexi and crew. I ended with Lexi's pique with the news that the police department was not taking a serious look at what Lexi's posse had uncovered.

"So now, maybe the Buffalo cops will take a closer look at the connection," I said.

"Perhaps, but no one is telling the cops about the connection," Sheila said. "The feds are not convinced some elements of the police aren't involved in the situation."

"When I tell Lexi she'll hit the ceiling."

"Yes, she will. That's why you can't tell her."

"What? Are you crazy? She'll kill me if she finds out I knew and didn't tell her."

"That's why Colleen wanted me to get word to you. If she knew, there is a good chance she would do something rash and blow an investigation that could end up taking down some really bad people. You must promise me you will not breathe a word of this to her."

I pondered that for a minute, knowing that, once again, discretion would overrule valor.

"Okay," I said. "I promise but you do know she will hurt me if she ever finds out I kept this from her."

"You're a big boy, Coe. You can take the pain." She smiled and kissed my cheek again and stood, signaling to me our little tête-à-tête was over. I stood with her and let her give me a hug far gentler than Eddie's.

I winked at Vera on the way out and accepted her sneer in return. I made it to my car, wondering how I would keep something like an FBI caper a secret. Maybe I should tell her, I thought, after swearing her to secrecy. But the more I thought about that idea, the less I liked it. Semantically, Lexi Crane might be a proper noun but practically, she was a verb – an action verb; not likely to take information about bad people lightly and less likely to not do anything about it. Sheila was right. I'd just have to take the pain. I drove to my spot under my building and walked up to the lobby. Simon was there to greet me.

"Miss Marsha would like to see you, Coe. She said to be sure I told you as soon as I saw you so it must be important."

I was tempted to tell him that every request from Marsha was to be deemed important, but I thought he probably knew that. I took the elevator to her floor. Her door was open, but I knocked anyway.

"Hello ... Marsha, it's Coe. You wanted to see me?"

She came into the hallway looking as though she's just walked a Fashion Week runway, as always. She was the only woman I knew who could make jeans look like formal wear.

"Shall I make tea?" she said.

"Sure," I said, following her into the kitchen.

"Simon indicated your ribs are healing well."

She caught me off-guard with that one. How would Simon know about my healing? I quickly realized, though, that he had seen me running and assumed the rest.

"I see Simon's role around here extends beyond opening doors and greeting guests," I said, "but he's correct. The ribs are much better. I may even get back to my running regimen soon. But I doubt you wanted to see me about that."

"No need to get touchy," Marsha said. "Simon keeps me abreast of things around here and I'm grateful for that."

No one had a more accurate finger on the pulse of this city than my mother, so the only thing she needed Simon for was filling her in on my comings and goings.

"Go sit on the terrace," she said. "Let's enjoy some of this spring sunshine."

I went out and sat on a patio chair that was more comfortable than any I'd owned when I worked for the mayor. I looked out over the eastern panorama of Buffalo and noted the seventeen-story tower of the Central Terminal still dominating the view. That's where it all changed for me but it still loomed sinister and foreboding, it's demolition delayed yet again. Marsha soon emerged with a serving tray carrying a fine tea service with floral pattern in dark blue.

"Is that a new tea set?" I asked, knowing she'd be pleased that I noticed.

"It is … beautiful, isn't it? It comes from the Czech Republic and I find it useful for everyday use."

Only Marsha would consider fine bone china fit for "everyday use" but that's my mother.

She poured and I related details of my conversation with Sheila.

"I hope you will honor her request for secrecy," she said.

"Of course I will honor my promise," I said. "You seem to have a very low opinion of me these days, mother." She is not fond of me calling her that.

"I have the highest regard for you, Coe, and you know that. What I question is your impulse control. You have a marked tendency to respond viscerally to various situations. You have an instinctual need to do so."

"Really? I have a tendency toward action and reaction, but I would hardly call that problematic."

"Perhaps you've forgotten about the nose you broke while working for the mayor or your response to it: self-exiling in Mexico rather than considering alternative responses."

Oh yeah … that, I thought. How many times is that singular act going to rear its ugly head?

"Point taken," I said.

"Good. Self-awareness is the first step toward self-improvement."

I thought that was a bit much but let it slide. There was little upside in arguing with the woman responsible for such improvements in one's life. We drank in silence for a bit then my mother dropped the bomb.

"Your father is coming up from Florida for a few days," she said. "He called earlier today and told me he wanted to see you and Eddie Murray and me, of course."

I smelled a rat.

"Are you sure you didn't call him?" I asked.

"Why ever would I do that?"

"Because you thought he might be enlisted in your quest to save me from myself. I gave Sheila my word about the investigation. I told you I would back off my own pursuits … pursuits I started because I was trying to help a couple of people in trouble – something I've done most of my life. But that doesn't seem to be enough, does it? I have to be molded into something or someone who meets your standard."

I took a few steps toward the terrace railing.

"Coe …"

"Let me finish, mother," I said. "I appreciate all you've done for me. I recognize your concerns for my safety, and I am even appreciative of it. You have given me a life I thought I would not have after my fiasco in the mayor's office. But you have to understand who I am and what motivates me. I am not some un-caped crusader seeking out trouble. I was thrust into this mess because a soldier and his sister were in harm's way. Now that they are out of that danger, I can stand down. I am not singlehandedly trying to rid Buffalo of crime. I just wish you would understand that and be even a little supportive."

"Now, are you finished, son?"

I answered by resuming my place at the table.

"My concern for you is predicated on one thing … your safety. That's the sum and substance of it. You are a fine man, Coe, and you have a wealth of experience both good and bad to guide you. But past success is not always a predictor of future triumph. You are wading in water much deeper than you think. That water is treacherous beyond your imagination. The confidence that makes you such a formidable individual can also blind the threats coming at you."

Marsha paused to sip her tea. I wanted to jump in with my own take on things, but her stare made me think silence might be the best option.

"You have done good work for the Norton twins," she said, "but that wasn't enough for you. You had to seek retribution and put yourself in danger needlessly. There are forces that can be brought to bear to further the campaign against the people who are breaking the law. You are not among those forces. You have the desire and the determination, but you don't have the tools or the numbers to do the job. If you are honest with yourself, you will recognize that. You and Eddie Murray do not constitute an army.

"I am afraid that all you have done with your latest attack is stir up the hornet's nest and put yourself squarely in the focus of those who would do you harm. You are still recovering from the damage they inflicted already, and I know you well enough to know you are not about to let the bad guys land the last blow. That's why someone called your father and that's exactly why he's coming up here."

Marsha leaned over and took my hand in hers.

"Coe, I wanted desperately to be part of your life because I knew there was such good in you. Everything you've done since you've been back in Buffalo has proven that out. The help I provided you in the Central Terminal adventure would have been meaningless if you weren't so bright and intuitive. I've tried to give you the life you deserve, a life of comfort that would give way to a life of accomplishment. Please don't risk that to satisfy your sense of chivalry."

We sat like that for some time, my hand wrapped in the warmth and softness of hers. She had made some interesting points and she seemed to know me better than I knew myself. I hated when she did that. I wasn't quite ready to abandon my desire to rid my city of the Loading Dock, but maybe it was time to let others finish the job.

"When does Dad arrive?" I said, finishing my tea.

"Tomorrow morning," Marsha said, "and he's expecting you to pick him up at the airport."

CHAPTER EIGHTEEN

My FATHER'S FLIGHT WAS on time. He'd been living on the west coast of Florida for a few years. The punishment he'd endured in Vietnam and the subsequent arthritis and other afflictions made winter too painful. He was kind of a legend in town, having been a well-known and respected reporter. He didn't look a whole lot different than the last time I saw him when I enlisted his help in our Central Terminal caper. His tan was deeper and he looked to have lost a little weight. He approached me tentatively and finally extended his hand.

"I suppose a hug is out of the question," he said.

"Wow. Bad news travels fast."

"It's Buffalo, kid. Any news travels fast."

We waited for his luggage, making small talk. He got his bag and we went into the parking garage and found my car.

"Nice ride," he said, looking the Audi over.

"Life is good," I said. "Last year made a big difference in my life."

"Yeah, I heard about that. Good for you. How's that sweet Lexi of yours?"

"Still not as much mine as I would like but she's doing great."

I headed for the exit and suggested we stop at Shaughnessy's for a visit with dad's bestie, Ed Murray.

"Murman would never forgive me it he wasn't our first stop," dad said. So off to South Buffalo we went.

"Catch me up on things," he said, and I filled him in on the most important details of our efforts to help the Norton twins. I omitted any mention of my last visit to the Loading Dock, assuming Marsha had filled him in as part of the urgency in getting him up here. Fifteen minutes later, we pulled into the lot at Eddie's place.

"Damn," dad said, "looks like Eddie is doing all right for himself."

"He's got a great spot here and runs it well. Does he know you are in town?"

"I told him I might be headed this way but didn't give him any details, so no, he doesn't know."

This should be good, I thought. We walked in and I called for Eddie in a loud voice.

"Murray! Someone is out here threatening to kick your ass!"

Eddie emerged from the kitchen still in his apron and armed with a tiny baseball bat, looking like he was ready to go to war. He took one look at my old man, dropped the bat, and threw the apron away. The two of them engaged in a bear hug that hurt my ribs just looking at them. When they broke it off, we took stools at the bar, and Eddie summoned his bartender, Alyssa.

"Give us three Buds, darlin', and keep them coming."

It didn't take long for the two of them to start down memory lane, reminiscing about the bad old days in Vietnam. They didn't serve together and only became buddies after they returned, but they both were immersed in the blood and fire of that shitty war; so immersed that it took the support of each other to make their way out of the psychological residuals of combat. They went on for a full fifteen minutes without even looking my way, but I didn't mind. It was great to see such friendship. Eddie only noticed when I signaled Alyssa for another beer.

"Hey Josh, did the kid tell you about our last incursion into bad guy territory?" Murray said.

"No, he didn't, Ed. He must have forgotten. Why don't you fill me in?"

I knew this wouldn't be good. I assumed the details would be seriously tortured in Eddie's telling of the tale but was pleasantly surprised until he got to the end.

"So this slob throws Coe out the back door and the kid hits the ground. Before anyone moved, two other slobs are around the kid trying to kick his ribs into mush. But then me and my guys wade in and drop the two while Coe recovers and knocks the other guy down. No easy job with your ribs on fire. Then, with the goon on the ground, Coe breaks the guy's jaw with one punch."

That tidbit drew a disapproving look from my father I'd seen a lot of when I was a kid but not much since.

"No, Mur, I hadn't heard that before. Must have been some punch, Coe."

"I think Eddie is overstating the punch and its effect," I said. "I did get a good one in though."

"You'll have to tell me more about it later, son. So what else is new in town, guys?"

We spent the next half an hour catching my old man up on the progress the city had made and continued to make, including the delay in demolition of Central Terminal.

"So that haste in searching the building last year wasn't needed at all?" my father said.

"I guess not but it was fun prowling around the building. I hope they can find a use for it and end the demolition discussion once and for all," I said. We chewed on that for another thirty minutes before Eddie called a halt to the reunion.

"Guys, I'm sorry to break this up but I have to go meet with one of my meat providers, but we'll pick it up again before you head back, Josh, okay?'

"Sure Eddie. I'm spending a week or so. We'll reconvene soon."

Eddie gave the old man a hug, started to give me one, but pulled back and shook my hand. My ribs were glad he did.

As soon as we got in the car, my father started in on me.

"Do you have any idea whose jaw you broke?"

"No, who was he?"

"How the fuck do I know? That's my point. I don't know who you are messing with and neither do you. You don't know if he was a wise guy or Russian mob or who he's connected with. You know better than to initiate hostilities without good intel. How many times have I told you to always know your enemy?"

"About as many times as you told me never leave a man behind!" I said. "These assholes, whoever they are, beat a GI within an inch of his life. The kid staggered to my door because he'd been told I would help him. So I helped him. I helped him the only way that made sense. I helped him because I didn't want to leave him behind."

My dad must have sensed how angry I was getting, and he eased up.

"Look, Coe, we are worried about you. We're worried what you've started might escalate out of your control. There are way too many variables to just wade into this like you and Eddie did."

We drove in silence for a few minutes, partly because I knew he was right.

"What does my mother know about the assholes at this phony night club?" I asked.

"She doesn't know anything," my father said. "That's why she's worried. She can usually get a handle on things quickly in this town but this time she's drawn a blank."

Now I knew why everyone was nervous. If Marsha couldn't identify the enemy, she sensed they might be more trouble than we thought. Well, more than I thought anyway. I hadn't really thought about it at all. I sensed we needed a lot more reasoned discussion on this, so I changed the subject.

"Are you bunking with me?"

"No, your mother has a guest room and more room in general so I'm staying with her while I'm here."

"How long are you staying?"

"That's to be determined," he said. "Your mother is convinced you are getting in over your head. I agreed to come to convince her you could take care of yourself but as she told me more I started leaning toward her viewpoint."

"I've already told Marsha I would back off. I don't know what more you want me to do."

"It appears you've told her that before with some flexibility in your commitment. Let's talk this over and see what needs to be done and who is best equipped to do it."

We reached West Ferry and I stopped at Simon's station before entering the underground garage.

"Hey Simon, come here and meet my father. He's in town looking for a job as a concierge."

Simon approached the car absent the self-assured smirk that was part of his persona.

"Hello, Coe's dad," he said. "Welcome to Buffalo."

My father caught on and played along.

"Thanks, kid. Keep your ear to the ground about possible jobs, okay?"

"Sure thing," Simon said, heading back to his hut.

We parked, got my father's luggage, and headed for the elevators.

"Tell me again, for the first time, why we did that," he said.

"Simon is a basically good guy but, he needs his chain jerked occasionally."

A minute later, we were at Marsha's door and my phone rang. It was Lexi. I let my father hug my mother while I stayed in the hall.

"Hey, I was going to call you," I said. "My father's in town and I want to take him and Marsha to dinner tonight."

"I need dinner or a drink or something," she said. "I am so pissed off I can hardly think straight."

"Well, save the thinking for later. My mother brought my father in for little intervention."

"What the hell..."

"Save it," I said. "I'll pick you up at seven, but I'm driving tonight. I don't want my mother falling out of your Jeep."

She giggled and hung up.

···

Lexi and I weren't the only ones on the phone.

Dora was across the street from my building.

"Yeah, I'm sure it was him," she said into the phone. "He's driving one of those ring toss cars. You know, the one with the circles on the front. An Audi? How the fuck do I know? If an Audi has four circles on it, then, yeah, it's an Audi."

My parents sat in the back while we drove the ten minutes to Lexi's building. She was standing in front when I pulled up. She slid into the front seat and gave me a big kiss.

"Hi handsome, you smell good." Then she turned and smiled at Marsha and Josh.

"Hi, Coe's parents. You look great."

She definitely wasn't lying about that. My mother had an incredible ability to turn a blazer and slacks into a fashion statement while my father was tan and lean.

"Great to see you both," Lexi said. "It's been a while since I've seen you, Josh. Welcome to town."

"Great to see you, Lexi," he said. "Any luck reining in my son?"

"I'm his girlfriend, not a magician," she laughed.

"Where are you taking us Josh?" my mother asked.

"I thought we'd head south to the Mulberry. Lexi and I haven't been there in a while and the food is terrific."

I drove south over the Skyway bridge and along the edge of the old Bethlehem Steel plant, long dormant but now showing signs of reuse as warehousing facilities were sprouting up. As I made the turn to head to the restaurant, my father took notice of his surroundings.

"This is Bethlehem Park," he said. "I used to come out here to play basketball."

"Why all the way out here?" I asked.

"This is where the action was," he said, as we pulled up to Mulberry.

"Most of the kids who lived out here were black and they could really play. So, if you wanted to test yourself against the best players in the area, this is where you came. And by the way, this so-called restaurant used to be a crappy gin mill where the plant workers cashed their paychecks."

"Then it's come a long way," I said. "They have some of the best Italian food in the area."

We entered and were greeted by Tim and Joe, the proprietors. I made the introductions and we headed to a table in the back. We were getting settled in when my usual server appeared.

"Coe," she said, kissing my cheek, "it's been too long since we've seen you. And you too, Lexi."

"So wonderful to see you again, Brenda," Lexi said, with more than a hint of sarcasm in her voice. Lexi doesn't like anyone else kissing me, even on the cheek.

We gave Brenda our drink order and waited until she returned with them to start talking.

"Marsha, I love seeing my father and love it even more to see him here in Buffalo, but I think bringing him here was overkill. I am not about to do anything crazy or stupid or anything else. I did what I did because those goons beat the shit out of a soldier who was trying to look out for his sister."

I took a swig of my beer and continued.

"After what the same goons did to his sister, I would think I would be more than justified in more retaliation. In deference to you, though, I promised I would stand down."

Marsha sipped her wine and took a long look into my eyes.

"Coe, you have injected yourself into something that is evil and ugly. No matter how pure your motives, you have put yourself in danger not just by attacking the thugs but doing it on their own turf. You've got to learn how and when to pick your fights. You want to lash out at the bad guys, but you must manage that impulse."

Out of the corner of my eye, I thought I could see Lexi rolling her eyes. She had less anger management than I did. Before she could interject, my father jumped in.

"Look, kid, I know where you are coming from. I really do. But your mother has a point. You acted without good intelligence on who you are attacking. We don't know who these guys are or what they are capable of, so you really do need to take a few steps back and let the authorities take over."

"The brass are dragging their feet," Lexi said. "My contacts in the department tell me they aren't taking what we do know seriously. They aren't prepared to do anything more than the bare minimum. Meanwhile, there are probably a lot of girls being abused the same way Jennifer Norton was abused and almost killed."

Lexi took a long drink from her beer and continued.

"My only problem with what Coe did was that he left me out of the play."

That earned me a punch on the arm.

My mother was not pleased and let us know it.

"You two are acting like children," she said. "You can't right every wrong with mere good intentions. And Lexi, kindly stop that annoying tactic of punching Coe's arm.

"Lexi's police contacts have already made a connection between the crews ransacking abandoned houses and the night club. My sources tell me there is a real possibility that there is an eastern European, possibly Russian, flavor to all this. If that is the case, you and all who try to stop them are in real danger. You are confronting an enemy far more treacherous than the street punks you took on at Central Terminal."

Brenda reappeared to take our food orders and that put a hold on the conversation. When she left, I wanted to put the entire issue to rest.

"Marsha, I have given you my word that I am off the case. Now, might we just take me at my word and enjoy our dinner?"

I'm not sure if my mother bought that but she gave me a slight smile. I knew we were on to a pleasant evening when my father winked at me.

"Hey Coe, is that waitress married?"

"I think she's hot for Coe," Lexi said, punching me in the arm and sticking her tongue out at my mother. That got a laugh from Marsha and the night only got better from there.

If anyone ever left Mulberry hungry, it was because they came only to drink. The food was delicious and served in proportions that gave a reason for all the Buffalo Bill jerseys lining the walls. Anything we couldn't eat, Lexi boxed up and took with her. We said our goodbyes and were making our way past the bar when Jim, the bartender, motioned to me. I leaned over the bar to hear what he had to say.

"Is that really your dad?" he said. I allowed that he was.

"He's hitting on Brenda."

"I thought he might. He came up from Florida to make sure I was walking a righteous path."

We both got a laugh out of that.

We pulled into our building and went to Marsha's apartment for a nightcap.

"Thank you for a wonderful dinner, Coe," Marsha said, "and thank you for your assurances of your safety."

Marsha and Josh were sipping brandy while Lexi and I stuck with Budweiser. We clinked glasses and bottles and I said "to safety. We finished our beers and Lexi and I took our leave. Riding down on the elevator, I asked Lexi if she wanted me to drive her home.

"If you wouldn't mind, handsome. I'm stuffed from all that lasagna. I feel like the boa that just swallowed a piglet."

"Your wish is my command," I said, wishing I could wake up next to her.

I pulled out of the underground garage and headed to Lexi's. I started to turn onto Delaware Avenue when I thought I saw Dora the ingrate sitting on a lawn across from my building. Seems strange, I thought, but everything about the girl was strange.

CHAPTER NINETEEN

I stopped at the light and pointed out the kid sitting on the grass.

"A little late for a picnic, isn't it?" Lexi said.

"That's the piss pot who started all this," I said. "She was the one who started me looking for the Norton girl in the first place."

"Hell yeah it is. I forgot to tell you Lindsay saw her on Elmwood handing out cards for the Loading Dock."

The kid saw us looking at her and she got up and started running.

"What the hell?" I said. "We've got to check her out and see what she has to do with this stuff."

"So you lied to your parents?" Lexi said.

"No, I didn't lie. I said I wouldn't do anything dangerous. Finding out what this kid's role in all this isn't dangerous."

"What did you make of all that talk at the restaurant?"

"I'm more than a little pissed off," I said. "I told you the story of how my old man and Murray wasted the debt collector for the bookie back in the day, right?"

"Yeah, you did, and you told me what they did to that city auditor they tracked down in Florida. Your dad is kind of scary."

"Kind of, my ass. He and Murman were a two-man wrecking crew and now he comes up here to scare me off the assholes at the Loading Dock. He and Marsha still think of me as a kid and I'm not happy about it."

We pulled up in front of Lexi's building on Ellicott Street and she leaned over the console and gave me a big wet kiss.

"Thanks for tonight," she said. "I really had a good time."

"You just liked hearing me take shit from my parents."

"Well, there was that and the food wasn't bad either." She gave me another kiss and went inside carrying her doggy boxes. I pulled away recognizing what a lucky guy I was.

•••

I got up in the morning enjoying the sunlight beaming through my French doors. Spring was definitely making an appearance. All that warmth was too much to waste, so I put on my running clothes and headed downstairs. Simon was standing outside, face toward the sun.

"What's happening, Simon?"

"Just loving this sunshine," he said. "Hey, you weren't serious about your old man coming up here to live, were you?"

"Nope. Just jerking your chain a little. He's only here for a little while."

"That's good news. I had nightmares last night about him taking my job."

"That was the idea. Simon. Hey, have you seen a scruffy looking girl hanging around lately?"

"There was a girl over there across the street a couple of days ago. If you washed a few layers of dirt off her, she might be passable. Why? You looking for a little strange action?"

"Simon, that's the kind of shit that will one day get you fired. I saw her hanging around on the lawn near the corner and just wonder what she's doing around here. I used to see her up on Elmwood."

Simon looked over at the lawn across the street.

"Maybe she thought the grass was greener over here." He laughed at his little joke. I didn't.

"Let me know if you see her hanging around." I took off toward Delaware Avenue and Forest Lawn. My ribs felt good and the sun was making me feel like I could run all day. There was a slight downhill toward the cemetery and I was running hard. It was going to be a good day ... maybe.

The grimy girl was watching from behind some shrubs across the street from my building. She pulled out her phone.

"He just left. No, he's running up Delaware toward the cemetery, the big cemetery at Delaware and Delevan. I don't know the name of the place. It's a goddamned cemetery! You can't miss it."

By the time she was ending her call, I was passing the circle at Lafayette and feeling strong. I entered the big gate and waved to the guide in the gatehouse and powered up the road leading to Scajaquada Creek. I crossed the bridge over the creek and headed north to the upper limit of the cemetery and looped around to the east side of the property and back down south to the Field of Valor. I stopped there, as I often do, to walk among the stones and read the names. I said a prayer and headed back to the road. As I did, I saw a white van idling on the roadway. I headed back toward Delaware Avenue, glancing over my shoulder to see if the van was still behind me. I didn't see it and thought I was being paranoid – until the van came around a corner following my path. I ran down to the gatehouse and went inside. The guy manning the house asked if I was okay. I saw the van retracing my route until I went into the building. Then, it made a sharp right turn and drove away quickly.

"Oh yeah, I'm fine but I was wondering if you saw that van come into the property?"

"Sure. It came in a bit after you came through the gate," the man said. "I remember because the driver looked at me and said 'map.' I found that a little rude."

"Thanks," I said. "I'll be back this way tomorrow." I gave him a wave and headed back down Delaware back to my building. Fifteen minutes later, Simon waved me down.

"Hey Coe, that street chick you were talking about popped up just after you left."

"She's not still there?"

"No man, she headed toward Elmwood."

"Thanks, Simon. Call me if she comes back, okay?"

"You got it."

I didn't bother stopping at my place but went right up to Marsha's. I rang the bell but got no answer, so I went back down and left her a message about the strange van that seemed to be following me. I showered and got dressed and called my sister.

"Hello, Coe. What can the Historical Society do for you today," she said.

"Might the HS know where my mother and father might have gone off to?" I asked. "I went up to her place to give her some news about being followed by an old white van while I was on my run through Forest Lawn, but she wasn't there. I did leave her voice mail though."

"Believe it or not, mother and your father have gone to Niagara Falls for lunch," Sheila said.

"Oh dear, I hope they aren't planning a honeymoon." That got a laugh out of Sheila.

"I never thought of that," she said, "and now I am sorry you put that notion in my head. Now tell me about your tail in Forest Lawn."

I gave her the rundown and mentioned that Dora, the urchin, had been spotted around my building.

"Do you think the two events are related?"

I filled her in on my first encounter with Dora and Lexi's cop friend seeing her handing out flyers for the Loading Dock along Elmwood Avenue.

"Hmm ... now what do you think is irrelevant?" she said. "The two things are not coincidences. They are definitely related. You might think about staying home until we can sort all this out."

Sheila picked up the thread from last night; that I wasn't capable of taking care of myself.

"Not a chance," I said. "I'm not going to get spooked by some scruffy girl and a white van. Kindly tell Marsha I called." I ended the call before I said something to Sheila I might regret. I called Lexi but got her machine.

Lacking alternatives, I decided to head to Cole's for lunch. Food might be involved but not necessarily. I was still stewing about all the people in my life assuming I couldn't handle myself. I was starting to wonder if I wasn't better off before the Central Terminal caper but given my new financial status, I dismissed that notion. I was definitely better off today but I could do without so many intrusions into my life. I went down to the garage to get my car. Ten minutes later, the car was parked on Elmwood and my butt was parked on a stool at the bar. I shot the shit with Donny Joe for a few minutes, catching up on some news around town and DJ's laments about bad beats he was taking in early season baseball.

"Don't lose your bankroll before Memorial Day," I said.

"Now you tell me," he said, heading to the other end of the bar to take care of other customers.

I was on my second beer when Shamus Culhane came in. It took him a full ten minutes to get down the bar to me after saying hello and sharing a laugh with virtually everyone in the place.

"You just can't stop campaigning, can you?" I said.

"It's in the blood now," he said, slapping me on the back. "What are you doing now, Coe, besides watching your investment grow?"

"Not much," I said. "Working out, trying to corral Lexi … you know, the usual."

Shamus laughed and we settled into a long conversation about local and national politics. Then he changed the subject.

"Didn't you ask me about some joint called the Loading Dock a while back?"

"Yeah, I did, and you were remarkably unhelpful," I said, smiling.

Shamus slapped me on the back again.

"Well maybe I can be a little more helpful now," he said. "Some strange shit going on over there."

"Strange in what way?"

"You remember Luther Butler, right? I was going to make him a Deputy Commissioner in the police department."

"I do remember. He backed out because his wife took ill, as I recall."

"Well, he told me they had a number of tips about some weird shit going on at the night club, so they were going to stage a surprise inspection of the place. You know, looking for code violations and shit but hoping to find more serious stuff."

"How did that go?" I asked.

"That's the thing," he said. "It didn't go at all. When the cops got there, the joint was closed."

"What night did they pick for this inspection?"

"A Wednesday and that's usually a busy night for bars in this town."

"That's weird. Who the hell closes on a random Wednesday night?"

"That's just what Luther said. Of all nights to close, it just happened to be a night the cops were going to show up. He thinks it's pretty strange."

I thought it very strange as well but didn't wish to share that with Shamus just yet. Lexi and her friends were pissed because they couldn't get the BPD brass to take them seriously about the Loading Dock and the night someone decides to take it seriously, the place is strangely closed. Something didn't smell right. I finished my beer, bought one for Shamus and some of his pals, and went outside to call Lexi with the new intelligence I'd just picked up. I called but got her machine again, so I left her a little teaser about some strange doings at the Loading Dock. I figured that would pique her interest. I headed back home to see if Marsha and my dad were back from their trip to the Falls. I pulled into the driveway and beckoned Simon over to my car.

"Simon, has Marsha returned yet?"

"They got back an hour ago but your father left a little while ago in her car."

That was probably good news. Marsha was the one I want to brief anyway as she knew all the players. I went straight to her apartment. When she answered the door, I was blown away yet again at how elegant a woman could look in jeans and a blouse.

"How was the Falls?" I asked.

"Your father has an affinity for the cataracts," she said, "but you know how it is when you live here, you take it for granted. But you didn't come up here to ask me about Niagara Falls, did you?"

"Ah, you know me too well." She took me to the sofa. We sat and I talked, filling her in on what I'd just learned from Shamus. She gave me her dubious look, but I shut that right down.

"Before you say anything, this is information that fell into my lap unsolicited. I wasn't searching around for it. Shamus was the one who brought it up."

She still had her dubious face on.

"And Shamus knew of your interest how exactly?"

I started to defend myself, but her smile indicated I didn't have to. She sat quietly for a minute before speaking.

"You're right, Coe. Something doesn't seem right about this situation. No owner would want to close on a traditionally busy night unless there was something more important than money in the works; something like avoiding scrutiny. Who was Culhane's source?"

"An inspector named Luther Butler. Shamus was going to make him a Deputy Commissioner at one time."

"I've heard of him and heard good things about him. That was one of your former boss' best qualities. He was a good judge of character. Who else knows about this development?"

"You are the only one I've told but I did call Lexi to give her a head's up."

"You indicated previously that her friends in the department saw a reluctance on the part of the higher-ups to give this appropriate weight. That reluctance and the development you just related might indicate a pattern and one I hope isn't the case.

"Tell Lexi the new information. Perhaps her police friends can weave some other threads into the situation."

I welcomed that. I knew what kind of ire keeping Lexi out of the loop on something like this would generate. My arm could use the break.

"Please keep me informed, Coe," Marsha said, rising. "But remember your promise to keep your distance from this tawdry business."

I kissed her cheek and went down to my place to call Lexi again, but I got her machine for the third time. It seemed like things were starting to take shape, but I still couldn't make out what shape that might be. I went out to the terrace to take in some of the warmth of the day and wait for Lexi to return my call. Far to the west, I could see the sun lighting the shimmer off the lake and the river with silver. Even from a distance, there was something soothing about watching the sunlight reflecting off the water. It must have been particularly soothing this day because the buzzing of my phone awakened me from an impromptu nap.

"Okay, Romeo, what's the big news that caused you to call during my lunch?" Ah, Lexi ... such a romantic.

"Who did you have lunch with?" I asked.

"Some old friends and a new one."

"New one? That's a little out of the ordinary for you, isn't it?" Lexi had a cadre of friends all of whom I could name. Most of them were friends from her days as a cop. Letting someone new into her group was a little unusual.

"What? You don't think I'm new friend material?" she said.

"I'll answer your question with a question. Is it a she, and is she a present or former cop?"

"Yes and no, in that order."

"How many non-cop women do you call friends?" Her silence gave me the answer. "I rest my case."

"Well, if you are going to be such a smartass, maybe I won't tell you why I made a new non-cop friend."

I told her my interrogation would stop and she proceeded.

"This woman has even more muscles than Lindsay and you know how buff Lins is."

It was hard for me to believe any woman could be more muscular and toned than Lindsay, but I let Lexi continue.

"It seems like this woman and her friend stopped in at the Loading Dock one night for a nightcap." Now, I was really interested.

"The two of them were at the bar and her friend went to the ladies' room. The Queen was scoping the place out ... "

"Wait, the chick is royalty?" I asked.

"Watch your mouth or I will tell her you referred to her as a chick and watch gleefully while she kicks your ass. Can I go on now or do you need more information?"

I couldn't tell if Lexi was miffed or was just being cute, so I took the safe way out.

"Please continue."

"Well, she's checking the place out but turns around just in time to see the bartender drop something in the friend's drink. She decides not to say anything until the friend gets back but after telling her friend what see witnessed, the friend is pissed, as you might imagine. So, she calls the bartender over and leans over the bar and throws the drink in his face."

"Wow, I like your new friend already."

"That isn't the best part," Lexi said. "The two are walking out and a bouncer puts his hand on the Queen's shoulder. That, apparently, is a big no-no for her. She snatched the guy's wrist with one hand and snapped his fingers backwards with the other.

"She thinks she broke at least two of the asshole's fingers."

I wanted to laugh but the more I learned about this place, the more serious the issues got.

"It's been a bad time to be a doorman at the Loading Dock," I said, reminiscing about my little foray at the place a week ago. I started to tell Lexi about my conversation with Shamus, but she was on a roll.

"You want to know why people call her the Queen?" she said. She didn't wait for my answer. "She belongs to Lindsay's gym, and everyone calls her the Queen of the gym."

"Does she look like a queen?" I said.

"She looks like a goddamned Playboy model." Lexi said. "She's drop-dead gorgeous. There were five of us at lunch, all girls of course, and I think three of them might have wanted to take a shot at her themselves. She's that good-looking."

None of Lexi's friends were inclined to pursue women to my knowledge and I didn't have the courage to ask if Lexi was one of the three.

"So what's your big news?" she said. "Some more dirt about the Loading Dock?"

I told her about my discussion with Culhane and what Luther Butler had told him about the inspection.

"Butler is a good cop," Lexi said. "Everybody likes and respects him. If he thinks something is fishy, it probably is."

"Forget about Butler for a minute," I said. "What do you think? Cat can't get her bosses to take her issues seriously and when they do, the place is conveniently shut down."

"What are you thinking?" she said, "that someone's tipping them off?"

"I'm just laying out some facts, Lexi, but doesn't it seem too convenient that the place was shut down the one night the cops decide to take a look? Now you tell me about your new friend and her encounter, which, by the way, gives evidence to what we found in the garbage at the place; the place where the Norton girl was last seen. You heard my mother say there is something evil and ugly about that place. I think it's even more evil and ugly than we thought."

"So what are we going to do about it?"

CHAPTER TWENTY

An hour later, Lexi and her friends assembled at my condo. She had briefed them on the curious circumstances surrounding the Loading Dock and they were not happy. The women on the force had not even heard of the failed attempt to get inside the place.

"This sounds like someone in the department might be playing on both sides of the street," Cat Redmond said.

"No reason for a supposed night club to close on a usually busy night unless they knew what was coming," Lindsay said, giving voice to what we'd all been thinking.

"We need to know if this was strictly a police deal or if anyone else was involved," Lexi said. I could see it in her face. She didn't want to believe a cop might have tipped the owners off.

"Let's be sure we know who was involved."

A new face in the group spoke up, a very pretty face. I assumed the speaker was the Queen Lexi told me about.

"I don't really give a shit who was involved," she said. "Those assholes are drugging girls and I think it's time we taught them a lesson."

The women all started talking at once and I took the opportunity to introduce myself to the Queen.

"I'm Coe," I said. "Should I call you Queen or Queenie or something else?"

"I've heard a lot about you," she said. "It's always nice to put a face to the name. My real name is Agatha, but I am not particularly fond of it or Aggie or any other derivation. Some smart ass at the gym thought he was being cute by calling me the queen of the gym. But after putting him in his place, I decided I liked being called the queen."

"I can relate," I said. "My given name is Jericho and I'm not particularly fond of that. So Queen it is."

I turned my attention to the rest of the group.

"Lexi, can I get you ladies something to drink?"

Five minutes and two empty wine bottles later, they resumed talking in earnest about steps to be taken. Still mindful of my commitment to my mother, I acted as bartender and stayed out of the conversation. Redmond said she would try to ferret out details of the failed BPD mission and report back. I offered to have some food delivered but there was scant interest. They were enjoying my wine, though. Two bottles later, the confab broke up. Only Lexi, Queen, and Lindsay remained.

"This is some sweet place, Coe," Queen said.

Lexi jumped in before I could answer regaling her new friend with the role my mother played in picking the place out and furnishing it.

"Damn, I need a mother like that," Queen said. "Really though, very nice indeed."

Lexi took the two women out to the terrace and showed them the effect of the setting sun over the lake. The three of them stood at the banister in silence, soaking up the view. When they came back in, Lexi started walking Lindsay and the Queen to the door.

"Lindsay, Lexi mentioned that you had seen that little Dora up on Elmwood," I said. "Could you keep an eye out for her when you are on patrol? She's been lurking around here for a while and I'd love to know what she's up to."

"Absolutely," she said. "Want me to bust her ass?"

"No, no. Just let Lexi or I know if you see her again. I can take it from there."

They left and Lexi and I moved to the couch. She took my arm and snuggled up to me.

"Thanks for being so hospitable," she said, "but I've never seen you this quiet before, especially when the talk is all about kicking some ass."

"You heard my mother the other night, right? I don't want to piss her off by lying to her, so I'm on the sidelines for this one, for now."

"Wow, she really struck a chord, huh? I've never seen you like this."

"When you knew me, I didn't have a mother and my father was down south. I must be getting old or something," I said. "She was so adamant about the threat; it makes me wonder if I'm missing something.

"But enough of that shit. Do you want to go to Pano's or some place?"

"I'm too comfortable on this luxurious couch your mother picked out. Let's just stay here for a while."

We did and when I woke up, Lexi was gone and the room was dark. Damn this comfortable furniture. I cleaned up and headed to bed, wondering when Lexi would break down and spend an entire night. I was in bed with MSNBC on the television when she called.

"You're awake," she said.

"You would have made a great detective, Lexi. Where did you go? I had big plans for tonight."

She laughed and I didn't know if that was a blow to my ego or if I'd said something funny.

"I could tell by the way you were snoring," she said. "What's the female equivalent of testosterone? Talking about trashing the Loading Dock got me all pumped up."

"The female equivalent is Chateauneuf-du-Pape," I said. "You and your friends drank five bottles of it this afternoon."

"Maybe that's why I feel so sleepy," she laughed. "Aren't you glad you can afford to buy another case of that stuff?

"I just called to say goodnight. You were sleeping so soundly; I didn't want to wake you."

"Well, it would be nice of you to whisper it in my ear instead of over the phone," I said.

That touched a nerve as I thought it would and she couldn't wait to get off the phone.

"Call me in the morning," she said. "We can do something tomorrow and I promise to be worth the wait."

She ended the call before I could respond. I fell asleep with Rachel Maddow giving her nightly seminar on the state of things in America.

•••

Her call woke me.

"Hey, handsome, I'm going to have breakfast with Cat. She got some info on the Loading Dock fiasco."

"Well then, I guess that relegates me to a run," I said. "Maybe we can have lunch then? We could take that nice drive out to Connor's or something."

"Sounds enticing," Lexi said. "I have good vibes about that place."

"Let me know when you are finished with Cat."

She blew me what sounded like a telephone kiss and clicked off. I set about finding some semi-clean gear to run in. The day was sunny, and it looked like a great day for a jaunt through Forest Lawn. I stretched and headed down to the street.

"Hey Coe, there were some fine chicks heading up your way yesterday," Simon said. "You got quite a harem."

"I think Lexi, for one, would take serious offense to that term," I said. "I thought I told you women don't like that stuff."

I figured throwing Lexi in there might emphasize the point as he had such 'feelings' for her. I gave him a wave and started off on my usual route, unaware I was attracting some unwanted attention.

"He's running up Delaware," Dora said into her cell phone. "No, I don't know where he's going. How could I? But I'll bet he goes to that big cemetery again. That's his usual spot."

The beautiful day had me hitting a good pace on the downhill from my building. I rounded Gates Circle and got to the gate of the cemetery in just over eight minutes. I waved to the guide in the gatehouse and started picking up my already quick pace but instead of running my clockwise route north, I decided to switch it up and run counterclockwise, roughly parallel to Delevan Avenue. I was feeling good, and my pace reflected that feeling.

But for those of you who have been reading along feasting on my witty repartee, I'm afraid that ends here. The rest of the story I learned second hand from Lexi, Marsha, and Sheila. For as I was sprinting passed the Field of Valor, ready to head north, the white van came into view. This time, though, the van wasn't behind me, it was speeding toward me and before the threat registered, the right front of the van threw me into the air and dumped me on the grass amid those righteous souls interred there. And that's it for what I can attest to. I was out cold with more than a couple broken bones and a head injury that I'm still recovering from so the rest of the story comes from Lexi and other sources.

CHAPTER TWENTY-ONE

"How the fuck long was he lying there?" Lexi said.

"No one really knows," Marsha said. "He entered the cemetery while only one person was on duty at the Delaware entrance. It appears Coe was struck near the Main Street entrance but no one was on duty there yet. A mother coming to put flowers on her son's grave and saw Coe in the grass.

"She said she thought he was a drunk student from Canisius College across the street tried to rouse him with her foot but when she saw all the blood, she called nine-one-one."

Lexi was with Marsha and my father at Erie County Medical Center waiting for an update from the doctors.

"I told the dumb ass to carry some ID with him when he ran," Lexi said. "How long was he here before you got called?"

"It was just a stroke of luck that one of the emergency room nurses recognized him," Marsha said. "She said she had stitched him up several months ago after some incident at the Central Terminal."

Lexi remembered it well. An old homeless guy living in the neighborhood around the Terminal whacked Coe with a two by four after mistaking him for one of the gangbangers that harassed him.

"The nurse told me he'd been a John Doe for about thirty minutes before she saw him," Marsha said. "She told one of the doctors who he was and he got word to a friend of mine on staff."

While the discussion continued, Coe's father sat in a chair with his face in his hands, saying nothing. Lexi looked over at him and asked Marsha if he was okay but Marsha looked away without speaking.

The wait continued when Lexi got a call from Cat Redmond.

"The investigators found a headlight rim from the vehicle they assume hit Coe," she said. "They will be joining you at the hospital to see if they can get any more clues from his clothes."

"But there were no witnesses?" Lexi asked.

"Nope. Thank God that woman found him because there's no telling how long he might have laid there."

"Well, his doorman said Coe took off about eight fifteen," Lexi said. "He usually runs a ten-minute mile and it's just over a mile to Forest Lawn so he would have been at the gate around eight thirty."

"That's helpful," Cat said. "We can check with the gatekeeper and see if he can give us an accurate time line. If we know when Coe was struck, we might be able to get a look from a security camera and see what kind of vehicle hit him."

"You don't need to review the cameras," Sheila said, moving quickly to join the group. "Coe told me about a white van following him through the cemetery just yesterday. So I'm sure that headlight rim will be from such a vehicle."

With that, Sheila gave Marsha a hug while tears welled up in her eyes while she spoke to her mother.

"Coe told me he tried to call you yesterday while you and Josh were at the Falls and he said he'd spotted some tattered girl who started Coe looking for the Norton girl," she said. "Then he mentioned the white van following him and I told him I definitely thought the two incidents were related and I think that now more than ever."

Lexi didn't wait for Sheila to finish talking. She'd heard enough. She took out her phone and speed dialed Lindsay. An orderly walking by told her cell phone use was not permitted in the hospital.

"Shut the fuck up," Lexi said and continued to speak to her friend.

"We've got to find that girl who was handing out the Loading Dock slingers. She might be the key to all of this shit." Lindsay asked how Coe was doing.

"He's not good," Lexi said. "Last I heard, he was being prepped for brain surgery and I don't like the sound of that. Tell the others we've got a mission and I'll see you when you get off."

She ended the call and approached my father.

"You and Marsha wanted him far away from this happy horse shit and now you got what you wanted but I better be able to count on you when the shit hits the fan."

Josh raised his head and gave Lexi a look that scared her.

"Whenever, however, whatever it takes to get the bastards who did this to my son."

A doctor appeared and started speaking to Marsha. She stopped him and beckoned to Josh to join her. Lexi, Sheila and Cat watched the discussion anxiously. The doctor stepped away and Coe's parents joined them.

"Coe has a broken left leg just below his knee, a broken wrist on that side as well, some serious bruising to his ribs, ribs that were just beginning to heal," Marsha said, "but the worst injury was to his head. The doctors are performing a CT scan now to determine what part of the brain has been affected."

Tears welled up in Sheila's eyes as she heard the news.

"Is he going to survive?" she said.

"The doctors are optimistic," her mother said. "They are concerned that there is bleeding on the brain. If the tests verify that, they may need to perform a procedure to drain that blood. In the best case, a simple hole is drilled in the skull and the pooled blood is allowed to drain."

Sheila let out a gasp and Josh put his arm around her shoulder.

Marsha continued.

"He may be placed in a medically induced coma to allow his brain to rest and the swelling go down."

While Sheila was on the verge of a meltdown, Lexi was on the verge of eruption. Her hands kept closing into fists and releasing and closing again. Cat noticed her friend's mood.

"What's our play?" she said.

Marsha overheard Cat's question and sensed that Lexi was on the edge. She approached the two women.

"Might I suggest that our play might be to think about this in calmer terms than we face now?"

"First of all," Lexi said, "who is *we*? You've been telling your son to stand down and walk away from the bullshit at the Loading Dock for more than a week. You even called his dad to come up and reinforce that opinion. 'Standing down' only works if the other side is standing down also."

"You are right, Lexi. I did want Coe to stand down. I did so not because he was wrong, but because I was afraid something like this might happen. Now that I've failed to stop that occurrence, I concur that it's time for action. I just want everyone to think about our response with clear heads."

That relieved some of Lexi's tension but not her grief. She started sobbing uncontrollably and Marsha took her in her arms.

"Coe is going to get through this," Marsha said. "He's tough and he's strong. He has the best people working for him here. Now, we need to get our best people working for him out there."

With that, Lexi pulled back and wiped the tears from her eyes.

"When do we start?" she said.

"Let's wait till Coe has undergone his surgery. Then we can start strategizing."

Josh joined the trio and put his arm around Marsha while taking Lexi's hand.

"Whoever did this will be sorry they fucked with the Duffys," he said. "For the time being though, let's just pray that Coe comes out of the surgery in good shape."

He kissed Marsha on the forehead and went back to his seat.

Marsha took Lexi's hand.

"We're going to stay here until Coe comes out of surgery," she said. "You two let the others know we've got some planning to do and we need all of their help. I'll call you tomorrow and let you know how the surgery went and when we can all get together."

Lexi didn't want to leave but thought Marsha's notion was best. She squeezed Marsha's hand and let Cat lead her to the elevator.

"I hope you are going to be my friend now, Cat, and not a cop because you might wind up having to arrest me if you are a cop."

"Don't worry about that," Cat said. "It's time we got some payback."

•••

Cat wanted to stay with Lexi but her friend said she'd be okay, so she went back to police headquarters to check for security camera footage that might have caught the vehicle. She figured the best chance would be cameras along Main Street but she'd check the cross streets as well.

When Lexi got to her apartment she called Lindsay who had already heard some of the news. She said the same thing to her as she had said to Cat. Lindsay knew she meant it.

"Can you call the Queen and let her know we'll be meeting up?" Lexi said.

"Sure. Can I tell her where? We don't want to be discussing our shit in public and Coe is out of the picture."

"I have a key to Coe's place but I think we will have an important ally in Coe's mom. She's good and pissed too. She wanted Coe to commit to letting things go and when he did it almost cost him his life." For the first time, Lexi got weepy. She wanted to show her mettle by keeping her composure but it was now all getting to her.

"Want me to come over?" Lindsay said, sensing her friend's grief.

"No, I'll be okay. Coe really got banged up though. He's having brain surgery now and has a broken leg ..." Reciting the litany of injuries started her crying again.

"I'm getting some of the girls and coming over," Lindsay said. "You shouldn't be alone right now." Lexi was too drained to protest. Thirty minutes later, her apartment was full of friends, booze, and food. The only one missing was Cat Redmond who was calling to check on surveillance cameras around the cemetery.

When the phone rang, the place went quiet. Lexi was reluctant to answer, dreading the chance the news was bad but when she did answer it was Cat.

"Good news," she told Lexi. "There is a camera at the college science building across the street from Forest Lawn and another at the metro station block away. The metro guys tell me they have a crappy white van speeding south on Main Street. I checked with the campus security guys and I'm heading up there to check their video."

"You might as well come by my place," Lexi said. "The gang's all here."

"A party and I wasn't invited; you bitch!" she laughed. "I'll be there as soon as I can."

Cat showed up an hour later with a big grin on her face.

"We got the bastards," she said. "The college surveillance camera not only got the van speeding out of the cemetery, it actually caught it hitting Coe. It was the same vehicle that the metro camera captured a few seconds later."

"Catch a plate?" Lindsay said.

"It didn't have a plate. The college video caught both front and back and the metro camera got the back. No plate front or back."

Lexi was running the new developments through her head. The security cameras would show the van deliberately struck Coe. The absence of license plates would prove premeditation. If she didn't kill the bastards beforehand, they would have a solid case. But she was intent on never letting the case go before a judge.

The crew all toasted Cat for her diligence in tracking the videos down. A few minutes later, the Queen caught Lexi in her kitchen getting ice.

"I didn't know your man, Lexi, but he made a great first impression," she said. "We're going to get these assholes and when we do, I promise I'll do more than break a few fingers."

Lexi looked into her eyes and knew she would. She knew they all would. This trash had been targeting women never knowing they would soon be the targets of women.

CHAPTER TWENTY-TWO

Lᴇxɪ ᴡᴀѕ ᴇᴍᴏᴛɪᴏɴᴀʟʟʏ ᴅʀᴀɪɴᴇᴅ, but she didn't have the heart to chase her friends out. She sat with a beer and smiled gamely at the encouragement they gave her but the only encouragement she wanted would come from the hospital. With little left to say, though, the women started drifting out. Only Lindsay and Cat were left when Marsha called.

"He's out of surgery," she said. "The doctor told me he was encouraged. There was some bleeding but not as much as they feared. They've drained it and are going to wait till morning to see how much of the swelling goes down. If all goes well, they won't have to medically induce a coma."

"That's good, right?" Lexi said. "No coma, I mean."

"Yes, Lexi, that's very good but we're still not out of the woods completely."

"I'll take whatever good news we have," Lexi said. "I've got Cat Redmond here and I'm going to put her on to tell you what she's discovered."

Cat gave Marsha a condensed version of her detective work in tracking down video of the van.

"That's great work, Cat," Marsha said. "We owe you."

"Not on your life," the detective said. "I'm a 'we,' remember. We're in this together."

She handed the phone back to Lexi.

"You have some terrific friends, my dear. Coe would be proud of all of them."

"Maybe," Lexi said, "after we restock his wine rack. He said we went through five bottles of his good stuff the other day."

Both women laughed, as much from the relief of the good medical news as from the depletion of his wine.

"What if we get together tomorrow at my place," Marsha said, "about five?"

"We'll be there," Lexi said, now on the verge of tears from joy. "We'll be there."

•••

When Lexi and her team convened at Marsha's condo the mood was upbeat as a result of the welcome news coming from the hospital. It changed, though, when Marsha addressed the reason they were there.

"We cannot allow this crime to go unpunished," she began. "It appears that the authorities are willing to wait and see at best and turn a blind eye at worst. We don't yet know if there is someone at police headquarters tipping off the thugs at the Loading Dock, but we should pledge that our conversations here remain confidential."

The women nodded their assent and Detective Redmond addressed the group.

"When this all started, when Coe and Lexi were looking for the Nortons, I told them to begin with what they knew, not search for things they didn't know. I am giving the same advice here. We catalogue what we know, and we expand on that to get to what we need to know."

Marsha and the others agreed, and they started offering items that Lexi wrote down on index cards. They knew the vehicle that struck Coe was a white van. They knew the board up crews that were ransacking houses drove a white van. They knew that Coe and Lexi had tracked the van to a building on the grounds of the old steel plant site where some of the stolen goods were unloaded. Sheila added the details she learned from Colleen Mayer about the FBI's findings at the storage site. That got her a quizzical look from Lexi. Lindsay added the piece about the sighting of the street waif on Elmwood handing out Loading Dock slingers and Lexi relayed that it was the kid's request from Coe that got the whole episode started. She added that the girl had been hanging around Coe's building lately, then added her discovery of the Ambien pill in the Loading Dock trash.

Marsha picked up the cards and started rearranging them. When she got them in the order she wanted she asked the group for their attention.

"Let's see how this all plays out. We know the Loading Dock is the center of all this illicit activity. We know the Norton twins were abused there. So we're on the mark in centering our attention there, right?"

The women nodded agreement and Marsha continued.

"This all began when the strange girl approached Coe on the street and fraudulently asked for his help finding a missing girl. Coe waded in with both feet but discovered the connection between them and that the girl lied to him. Without going too much further, I think that we need to find out what this strange girl knows about all this. She might not be essential to our work, but she might have some information that could prevent us from going in the wrong direction."

Lexi spoke up.

"I like that idea. How about Lindsay and I take that on? Lins, tell me when you are off duty, and we can prowl Elmwood."

"I'm on vacation for two weeks," Lindsay said. "I'm all in."

Marsha continued to pour over the index cards and was soon joined by Cat. A few minutes later, Marsha suggested they take a break while she headed to hospital.

"We can reconvene her about six? I'll have dinner catered for us and we can move our strategy along."

The session started to break up. Sheila joined her mother and Lexi approached them both.

"I probably can't get in to see Coe, could I?" Lexi said.

"I'm afraid not," Marsha said. "They haven't cleared him for visitors yet and when they do, it's usually just family but as soon as possible, I'll get the doctors to let you in."

"Thanks. I promise no arm punches when I see him."

•••

While the women were meeting, Josh traveled out to see Eddie Murray. After he listed all of Coe's injuries, Eddie threw the glass he was washing against the wall.

"Those coward bastards!" he said. "They needed a car to take Coe down? We need to teach them a lesson, Josh. This shit can't go unpunished."

"It won't," Josh said. "Someone is about to get a rude awakening. How many guys have you got?"

"As many as we need," Murray said. "I have nine guys from the UB football team working here and they can get more if we need them. We had two of them on our last escapade at that shithole."

"I don't know how many we need but it won't take a whole football team. At least I hope it won't," Duffy said, "but they tried to kill my boy, Eddie. He needed brain surgery yesterday to drain the blood off his skull."

Eddie smashed another glass, then he put his hand on Josh's shoulder.

"No more fucking around with these assholes," he said.

"No more fucking around," Josh said, and they started talking about how they would proceed.

•••

Lexi and Lindsay sat on a side street off Elmwood, waiting for a Dora sighting. They had driven up and down Elmwood a few times before deciding it might be better to just wait and see if she popped up.

"Just to be clear," Lindsay said, "are we going to kill anyone?"

"We won't but I might," Lexi said. "These pricks think they can come into town, terrorize our women, ransack abandoned houses, and damn near kill Coe?

"I won't ask you to do anything to jeopardize your job, Lins, but I don't have a job to protect."

"I wasn't asking because it was something I didn't want to do, honey. I asked because I just wanted to know how far we're going to go."

They waited for an hour before calling it a day. Lexi started up the Jeep and was about to turn on Elmwood when Lindsay spotted Dora.

"Over there, Lexi, by the church," she said, pointing.

"Well, I'll be damned." Lexi turned off the ignition and they got out of the Jeep. "Easy, Lindsay, let's not spook her." The little waif was hitting up passers-by for money but not getting much of a response.

"Let's grab her before she passes the church," Lexi said and Lindsay nodded, taking a pair of hand cuffs from her back pocket.

Dora was near the back of the building near a driveway that ran behind the church. When the two women approached, she held out a cigar box.

"Any spare change, ladies? I need a bus ticket to get back to Olean."

"Sure, kid," Lexi said, reaching in her pocket.

Dora extended the box toward her giving Lindsay the chance to slap the cuffs around her wrist.

"What the …" but before she could say anything else, Lexi slapped her hard across the mouth. "From now on, you speak only to answer questions. Got it?"

Dora started to protest but it was cut short when Lindsay punched her in the jaw. The two women dragged her off the street and behind the church. They had to drag her as she was woozy from the punch.

"Maybe I didn't make myself clear or maybe you're just stupid," Lexi said. "Nod if you understand the predicament you are in."

The little girl nodded her assent.

"You were scoping out my boyfriend for whoever the scum is you work for, and now he's almost dead in the hospital, so you are going to tell me everything I want to know or we might just need a bed for you next to him, understand?"

Dora started to say something, but Lexi's slap ended her effort.

"That wasn't a question, so you don't get to speak." The girl had blood leaking out of the corner of her mouth and her expression was one of terror.

"Who do you work for?" Lexi said, "and now you can talk."

"Some assholes who run that sleazy joint over on Exchange," she said.

"The Loading Dock?" Lexi said, and Dora nodded.

"Why were you spying on my boyfriend?"

"The dude in the ring toss car?" Dora said, "the car with the circles on the front?"

"Yes, that dude. Why were you spying on him?"

"Those dudes at the Loading Dock were pissed because he broke somebody's jaw, so they wanted to get back at him."

"Did you know they were going to kill him?" Lexi said.

"Kill him? Fuck no, I didn't know that. I just thought they wanted to rough him up a little."

"They tracked him to the cemetery and used that piece of shit van to damn near kill him," Lexi said. "Were you the one who told those guys where Coe liked to run?"

The terrified look became more a horrified look. She now knew her bosses had, indeed, tried to kill Coe and the two women in front of her were really pissed.

"Yeah, I guess I did ... but honest, I didn't know they would try to kill him ..."

Lindsay slapped her hard.

"Okay, bitch, we're going to take a walk over to my Jeep over there and you are going to tell us every fucking thing you know about the assholes who hurt my boyfriend. Is that clear? My friend is going to keep the cuffs on you so don't try to run. If you scream, make it good because it will be the last scream that ever comes out of your mouth."

Dora was between a rock and a hard place, but she figured her greatest danger was escorting her to a Jeep from which she might never exit. The fear of the Loading Dock crew was real, but it was remote. They were crossing the street when Dora risked speaking without answering a question.

"Are you going to kill me?" she said.

"Maybe," Lexi said, as they got in the Jeep, as Lindsay pulled a revolver from her waist band. "But if you tell me the truth and give us something we can use, we might just fuck you up a little. Do you know what your dickhead friends did to my boyfriend? He had brain surgery last night because his brain was bleeding. He's got a broken leg and a bunch of other shit wrong with him. So, I just don't know how bad I want to hurt you for setting him up.

"I would like to kill you for what you've done. Coe was trying to help you out and you stuck a knife in his back. You shouldn't have done that."

Dora was crying now.

"I know, I know," she bawled. "He was a decent guy but those goons at the club were really pissed after he broke the guy they call the Beast's jaw. And they said they would hurt me unless I told them where he went and when he went there. Please don't kill me. I'll tell you everything I know about those guys."

They sat in the Jeep for the better part of an hour and Dora hardly stopped talking to breathe. She'd aged out of the foster system and had nowhere to go so she jumped on a bus from Olean and wound up in downtown Buffalo. She sat around the bus terminal for most of a day and night when a guy approached her and asked her if she needed a place to stay. She was afraid to go with a black man but he seemed nice enough and that started the slide that landed her in bed with the Loading Dock crew. They didn't think she was pretty enough to pimp out, so they used her to recruit other girls at the bus terminal and off the street. She knew what to look for and she was good at picking out strays. The day she ran into Coe she was looking for Jennifer Norton. Jennifer had gotten away from the crew at the nightclub, and they wanted to find her before she could blow the whistle on them. Dora made up the story to see if anyone would help her find the girl. Coe took the bait. Lexi asked her about the doings at the Loading Dock.

"I know someone is drugging girls because I found a pill in the trash out back," Lexi said. "What do they do with them after that?"

"That was you who found the pill?" Dora said. "The guys at the place said a cop told them to be more careful about what they threw out."

"Wait, a cop told them?"

"Yeah, some dude they pay for information. I don't know who."

"Tell me what happens to the girls after they are drugged," Lexi said.

Dora described a hidden door somewhere they take the incapacitated women. If they were really good looking, they shot them up with heroin and they made them turn tricks at different functions around the area. If they weren't so hot, they let the dudes in the club use them. Dora was describing the horror so matter-of-factly, Lindsay was on the verge of beating the shit out of her. Lexi's continued questioning stopped her from doing it.

"Where do they keep the women after they shoot them up? They can't keep them at the Loading Dock, right?"

"No," Dora said, "they had some place where they drove them, but I don't know where. I was never at that place. I never even saw the girls at the club. They didn't want me going there."

Lexi drove the Jeep around for a while, getting more details from the girl before stopping at a fast-food place to get her something to eat. Dora ate three cheeseburgers, two orders of fries, and a milk shake.

"Were you hungry or what?" Lindsay asked her.

"I am starved," Dora said. "Those guys only give me twenty bucks a day and I have to pay Dante for staying at his place."

While Dora ate, Lexi gave her instructions. She was to go back to her normal haunts on Elmwood and do what she always did, with the exception of singling out women to be pimped. Then she gave the kid fifty dollars.

"If you breathe a single syllable about what you told me to the scumbags you work for, I will find you again and I promise you it won't be to feed you, understand?"

"Hell yeah, I understand," she said. "If I told them what I told you, they would save you the trouble of killing me. These are some really bad assholes."

Lexi dropped the girl off a few blocks off Elmwood so no one would see her getting out of the Jeep. Then they drove to Marsha's to share what they'd learned. As they drove, Lexi asked Lindsay what she thought.

"I think there is a sonofabitch at headquarters we need to castrate," she said.

"One mission at a time," Lexi said, "one mission at a time."

•••

When they arrived at Marsha's, Simon told them to go right up. Marsha was still at the hospital, but the caterers had already set up for dinner, Simon said, and she told him to send the team up when they arrived. He also told them not to wait for her to start eating. When Lexi and Lindsay got to the condo they were blown away. Denise Crawford was there already as was the Queen. A buffet had been laid out in the living room that could have fed the Buffalo Bills but neither woman had started eating.

"Ladies, Simon told me not to wait for Marsha to start eating," Lexi said.

"He told us the same thing," Denise said, "but this spread is too damned beautiful to disturb."

They were all laughing when Sheila arrived.

"Your mother doesn't scrimp, does she," the Queen said.

"Everything she does is over the top," Sheila said, as she started filling her plate with Caesar salad. "Don't let this get cold. Dig in."

That was the prompt the others needed as they put slices of tenderloin and fillets of salmon and grouper on their plates. Roasted potatoes and pasta were available to accompany the meat and fish. Sheila pointed them to a cooler full of beer, pop, water, and various juices. An array of wines was on the kitchen countertop.

"Mother only asks that you all maintain clear heads for the discussion," Sheila said. "Otherwise, drink hardy."

As they ate, Cat appeared along with an unexpected Colleen Mayer.

"Welcome, girls, help yourselves," Lexi said. "I didn't expect to see you, Colleen, but welcome aboard."

"Given what they did to Coe, I wouldn't miss the party for anything," Colleen said, "and that was before I saw all this food."

A new face appeared at the door, looking tentative.

"Hey, Ginna, thanks for coming," Sheila said. "Everyone, this is Ginna. She's a martial arts instructor at the gym I go to. Ginna, this is everyone."

One by one, the women took leave of the buffet line to introduce themselves to the newcomer. Lexi was one of the last.

"Great to see you again, Ginna," she said, "especially at a time like this."

"A time like this is why I came," Ginna said. "It's disgusting to know that women in our city are being treated like sex dolls. As soon as Sheila told me what the objective was, I was in."

The women ate and drank until Marsha showed up. She was smiling at the gathering and Lexi hoped that was good news. Marsha came to her first.

"Coe is awake but not exactly alert," she said, taking Lexi's hands. He's still groggy from the meds but the doctors say they are more optimistic than ever that he'll make a full recovery.

"And to compound the good news, Ron Norton was wheeled in to visit. Norton is recovering as well so that's more good news."

"What about his sister?" Lexi asked.

Denise Crawford interrupted.

"If I may," she said, looking at Marsha. "The Ambien and whatever else they gave her did their job. She has virtually no short-term memory. She told us at police headquarters her memory goes back to her search for her missing friend, then stops."

"I'm sure the hospital did a rape kit, correct?" Sheila said.

"They did," Marsha said, "and while it showed sexual activity, the woman was not pregnant and had no STDs."

"Then it might be a blessing she has little memory," Lexi said. "Who would want to know you were abused like that?"

Marsha poured a glass of wine and got the women focused. Lexi shared what she and Lindsay had gleaned from Dora, including the presence of a mole among the police.

"Goddamn it," Cat said. "It pisses me off to think someone inside the department is selling us out."

Denise calmed her down … a little.

"Take it easy," she said. "All we have is the word of a street kid who is probably getting her information second hand. The night of the supposed inspection, there was an agent from the liquor authority who was supposed to be with our guys, but he called in sick."

"Really?" Marsha said. "I have friends in that agency. Let me see what I can find out."

"The news about a secret door out of the club is interesting," the Queen chimed in. "I've been inside the place and just thought it was the long bar, the scattered tables and the dance floor. Where would a hidden door lead?"

Sheila opened her brief case and produced a large document.

"Every once in a while, the connection with the Historical Society has fringe benefits," she said. She unfolded the document and spread it out on the living room floor.

"The structure that houses the Loading Dock," she said, "was simply that: a loading dock. These warehouses ran all along Exchange Street, almost in a continuous structure. The trains stopped in the back and unloaded freight into the warehouses. Trucks pulled up to the loading docks facing Exchange Street and the freight was loaded on to them. Thus, the name 'Exchange Street.'

"But there isn't much separation between the different loading docks, so it is conceivable to punch a hole in a wall here near Michigan Avenue and another and another until you were a half mile or so down Exchange."

"So a storage room could have a hidden entrance to a dock next door," Lexi said.

"Or a restroom," the Queen said. My friend used the ladies room while we were there and said it was big but vacant. There were just a few stalls and a narrow sink and mirror."

"A restroom would make the most sense," Denise said. "If a woman was drugged and feeling woozy, the first place she'd go is to the ladies room. But if there was a hidden door, it wouldn't take much for someone to come in the john and grab the woman. She'd be taken out a separate exit so no one would ever see her being abducted. These fucking assholes thought of everything. They make me sick."

"They are probably feeling pretty confident about now," Lexi said. "They have a contact who's tipping them off. They had Dora keeping tabs on Coe. For all they know, they killed him and the Norton girl."

"Hmm … let's make them a little more confident," Marsha said. "Let's let them think Coe is in dire shape on death's door. They probably think of him as their biggest nemesis if they were so interested in getting him."

With that, she took out her phone and went into her bedroom. When she came out, she let them in on her idea. She called Coe's dad who still had contacts in the Buffalo media and had him use those contacts to publicize that Coe was on death's doorstep.

"That should make them think they have nothing to worry from him any longer," Marsha said. "Lexi, can you locate the waif you call Dora?"

"Sure," Lexi said. "Why?"

"Do you trust her?"

"A little … we scared the shit out of her and then we were nice to her. I think I can work her."

"Tell her to tell the goons they scared everyone off, that we found the Nortons and now our friend is going to die so we want nothing to do with them."

"Gotcha … we can do that," Lexi said, smiling.

Marsha suggested the women try the desserts before she gave them her ideas on how to proceed. When they finished, Marsha laid it out.

"As I see it, we have two issues," she said. "First is getting us all in the club at once without raising suspicions and second is finding out where they take the incapacitated women.

"Has anyone besides the Queen been in the club?"

No one had. Marsha wanted to count her out because she thought she might be recognized.

"No way, honey," the Queen said. "I'll have plastic surgery if I have to but I'm going in there and kicking some ass."

"Then we'll have to do something with that beautiful blonde hair," Marsha said. "It's not likely anyone would forget that, especially anyone whose fingers were broken."

That got a laugh out of them and then they settled down to develop a plan.

•••

About ten miles away, another group was discussing the same problem.

Josh, his buddy Murray, and a dozen of Murray's employees, were listening to a "special guest" at Murray's bar. Lexi's friend and former colleague, Brett Joseph was filling them in on some of the intelligence that other enforcement agencies had compiled about the Loading Dock.

"This stuff is being held pretty close to the vest, gentlemen, so I would prefer my name not be used as your source," the detective said. "It would seem some of the characters at the Loading Dock have attracted the attention of some federal agencies due to the background of the people running the place."

He went on to say that one Andrei Bychov was running the show. Gedeon Ustrashkin was his muscle and a couple of other Russians named Volkov and Gorky were also players.

"They all seem to be in the country legally," Joseph said, "but the feds can't find any record of them before they got here."

"What does that mean?" Murray said.

"It probably means they've reinvented themselves upon coming to this country. Their names don't track with any data that our agencies can find. Their passports and work visas seem to be valid but with the quality of counterfeiting these days, that doesn't mean they are. Oh yeah, there was a fifth guy – the guy Coe took out of commission, His name is Zolotov."

"There's just the five of them, then?" Josh said.

"There are a bunch more but they just seem to be working in other companies Bychov runs," the detective said.

"I'm thinking we get rid of these assholes with what we used to call extreme prejudice." Murman said.

"Not a good idea," Joseph said. "I don't know for a fact, but I think there is a lot of surveillance on the place. There's a better than even chance just bulldozing in there would be witnessed by some feds."

"All that surveillance didn't help my son," Josh said.

"Don't shoot the messenger," Joseph said. "I just don't want to see any of you jammed up needlessly."

"We got some intel that someone in the department is on the take for the Russians," Josh said, "but further information says it might be someone from the liquor authority. Can you check on your end?"

The detective looked pale.

"If it's someone on our team, I'll find out," he said.

The crew was mulling that news over when Josh got a call. When he saw it was from Marsha, he stepped away to take it.

"Good news about our boy," Marsha said. "He's still groggy and half out of it but the doctors are confident he'll make it all the way back. But that's only one of the reasons I'm calling." For the next ten minutes, she told him about the group meeting at her condo and what they were developing as next steps to deal with the Loading Dock. Then she asked Josh if he was alone. He told her where he was and why he was there.

"Oh God, Eddie is likely to firebomb the place," she said, only half in jest.

Then Josh told her about the information the detective was sharing.

"Part of what I have to tell you deals with the police," she said. "Can you come for dinner at my place? The women will be leaving shortly, and I had lunch catered. There is still a lot of food."

"Can I bring Murray? He'll be really jazzed if we leave him out of the equation."

"Sure, but tell him I don't have a lot of beer so if he wants some, he'll have to bring it."

Josh laughed and said he didn't think that would be a problem.

"We'll see you in an hour or so," he said, and went back to the bar. He thanked Joseph and watched him leave. Then he pulled Eddie to the side.

"We aren't the only ones strategizing," Josh said. "Come with me to Marsha's and let's hear what they've been talking about. She's got food but you need to bring the beer."

"Just point me in the right direction," Eddie said.

CHAPTER TWENTY-THREE

Before leaving, Lexi found out she was now cleared to visit Coe, so she was torn between finding Dora and visiting her man. Riding down on the elevator, she asked Lindsay if she could track down Dora and enlist her in their effort.

"Sure," her friend said, "I can bring Denise with me. She's good at persuasion."

Denise accepted so Lexi headed to the hospital while they headed up to Elmwood Avenue.

When she arrived, she was directed to the ICU. That took her by surprise after hearing only good news from Marsha. She was greeted by the charge nurse who calmed her fears a little.

"It's customary to keep a patient with his injuries here where we can keep a close watch on him," she said. "He'll probably be here another couple of days. You can see him, but he is in and out a lot, so don't expect he's going to engage in too much conversation."

Lexi was going to wisecrack that she wasn't interested in conversation, but she thought it might be too soon for jokes. When she got a look at Coe, she almost broke into tears. His head was wrapped in gauze and his face was badly swollen. His leg was in a cast and his left hand was wrapped in an Ace bandage. Add in the IVs, and the heart monitor and Coe Duffy looked like she's never seen him: beaten and vulnerable. Lexi went to his bedside and took his right hand in hers. Coe's eyes opened and he smiled slightly. She leaned down to put her face next to his. She held it there until she felt dampness on her cheek. She lifted her head only to see tears rolling down Coe's cheeks.

"Did I hurt you, baby?" she whispered. She was never one to use sweet talk and trite terms of endearment, but he looked so broken and helpless she could think of no other word for the occasion. Coe's smile said it all and he squeezed her hand. She put her cheek back on his and he closed his eyes. Her cheek got damp again, this time with her tears. She was even more resolved to strike back at those who did this to Coe.

•••

Lindsay and Denise sat in Lindsay's car on Elmwood Avenue. They waited about fifteen minutes before they spotted Dora dutifully handing out slingers for the Loading Dock. The two cops got out of the car when they saw her, but Dora looked at Lindsay and shook her head a little warning them off. The pair kept walking past her and headed into a coffee shop. They were on their second cups when Dora came in. She walked by and ordered a drink and sat two tables away from the women.

"They're watching me," Dora said, holding her drink to her mouth.

"Where are they?" Lindsay said.

"Don't bust them!" the girl said. "They'll know it was me."

"We don't want to bust them," Denise said. "We want to know what they're driving."

"Blue Ford, in the parking lot down the street."

Denise rose and left the shop and headed toward the parking lot. Lindsay went into her purse and pulled out a pad. Then she wrote the instructions as to what Dora was to tell the gang. Then she got up to head to the restroom but not before wadding up the message and dropping it alongside Dora's chair. When she returned from the ladies' room, Dora was gone but the note was still there but with a smiley face at the bottom. Lindsay snatched it up and went back to her car. Denise arrived shortly after with the Ford's plate number written on her hand.

"Missions accomplished," she said.

"We hope," Lindsay added.

Denise called Cat to check on the plate number. While she waited Cat ran it and told her it was registered to a corporation – New Enterprises, Inc. Denise allowed as how that didn't tell her much, but Cat told her the address listed for the corporation was on Exchange Street in Buffalo and in unison they said, "same as the Loading Dock."

•••

Lexi was a stew of emotions as she left the hospital. She was devastated to see Coe in such a sad state, happy that she got to spend time with him, and more determined than ever to make those who'd done this pay. She went straight to the gym to release her tension. Thirty minutes into her workout, Kevin approached her.

"Take it easy on my heavy bag," he said. "You're going to kick the stuffing out of it, literally."

Lexi took a break and toweled off some of the sweat. She told Kevin about Coe but not about who did it to him.

"Damn girl, I'm so sorry to hear that," he said. "I hope he makes a quick recovery."

"I just came from the hospital," she said, "and he's still not out of the woods but he's better than I thought he'd be." She renewed her assault on the heavy bag, driving kicks and punches and elbows into it in a frenzy, all the while picturing the blows landing on the goons who tried to kill Coe.

•••

"Hello Colleen. This is Sheila McCartan. I had a message that you called."

"I did, Sheila, and I think I have some news about the goons who were looting the abandoned houses. The FBI has taken three of them into custody." "Good for you, Colleen. I know this was a big case for you, but I have one more question, though. Were the men who were arrested of foreign descent?"

"Yes, they were, Sheila. All three were here on work visas from Russia."

"Thanks, Colleen, and congratulations on solving your case."

•••

"We were waiting for your call, Marsha," Josh said, beckoning to Eddie. "Sure, we can be there in half an hour."

When Marsha ended the call, Josh and Eddie gathered their team around the bar.

"We're heading up to Josh's ex," Murray said. "You guys hang tight. We'll get your assignments and let you know how this is all going to go down."

They nodded their collective assent.

•••

Lexi was in her Jeep when her phone rang. She checked the caller ID and answered it.

"Hey Maria, it's been a while. How're you doing?"

"I need to talk to you ASAP, girl. Can you meet me at Cole's?"

Lexi agreed but wondered what precipitated the call. She hadn't seen Maria Ramirez in months. Maria did her twenty years on the police force and retired. They had once trained together at KC's, but Maria was aiming to get in mixed martial arts fighting professionally. When she pulled up in front of Cole's Maria was standing in front. When she saw Lexi, she got in the Jeep.

"It might be better if we talk out here," Maria said.

"Sure … whatever. What's on your mind?"

"I heard about Coe," Maria said. "I want in."

"In on what, exactly?"

"Come on, honey. Cut the bullshit. I know you too well to think that you are going to let something like this slide. Whatever your play is going to be, I want in."

Lexi was stunned. There weren't many people who knew about Coe' injuries and fewer still, how he got them.

"And before you tell me you don't know what I'm talking about, I got the skinny from one of your besties. Don't ask me who, but it was someone you know and thought I might be an asset."

Lexi didn't bother with any denials or questions about Maria's source. It didn't matter who told her. Maria would be valuable to the mission. She gave Maria a fist bump and told her she'd be in touch with details. Maria gave her a hug before getting out. Lexi pulled away, mulling things over in her mind. The addition of Maria, maybe the best female fighter in Buffalo, gave her a strong team but she knew they would need more. There was no telling how many of these bastards would be in play, she thought. They needed to be ready for whatever came their way. She just hoped they could put together a plan quickly, before the goons folded their tent and moved on. She silently told herself they would not get away with what they'd done to Coe and their other victims. With nowhere else to go and not wanting to be alone, she called Marsha.

"Of course you can come by," Marsha said. "In fact, I was about to see if you might be available. We'll be joined by a couple other people."

When Lexi pulled into Marsha's driveway, Simon approached the Jeep.

"How's he doing?" he asked.

Lexi didn't want to show too much emotion.

"He's okay. He got messed up pretty bad but he's tough. He'll be fine in no time."

"Any idea who did this? Did they find the truck?"

"Nothing yet," Lexi said. "It just seems to be some random accident at the moment."

"You let me know if there's anything I can do, okay?"

She gave him her best effort at a smile and went inside. Marsha was waiting for her at her door. They hugged and Lexi let out all the emotion she'd been holding in, sobbing on Marsha's shoulder. Marsha let her get it all out, then stepped back.

"We have some work to do, Lexi, and you are going to have be one hundred percent if we are to succeed. Can you do that?"

Lexi took the handkerchief Marsha offered and got her composure back.

"You're damn right I can." Marsha touched her cheek and led her to the sofa. Once seated, Lexi told Marsha of her visit with Coe.

"I've never seen him look so helpless," Lexi said, again on the verge of tears.

"When I saw him, I thought he was Sikh, with his head all bandaged like that," Marsha said, getting a chuckle out of Lexi.

"What's the real deal?" Lexi asked. "I know you won't let the docs bullshit you. Is he really going to be all right?"

"Yes, he will. The doctors are confident his head injury will resolve itself in time. The surgery was successful in draining the blood and there doesn't seem to be any damage to the brain itself."

That assurance allowed Lexi to breathe again but Marsha continued.

"Right now, the orthopedic surgeons are concerned about Coe's leg. The fractures were severe and once the head injury stabilizes, they will need to operate on the leg. It would appear surgical pins, plates, and screws will be needed, and his recovery will take a long time."

"Those rotten bastards have got to pay," Lexi said.

"And pay dearly, my dear, but to insure that, we must plan effectively. Your friends will be essential but since we're attacking them on their turf, we'll need a to plan wisely." Marsha was interrupted when Simon buzzed.

"Coe's dad and his friend are here, Miss Marsha," he said. "Sending them up."

"That's why I asked Coe's father and Eddie Murray to join us," Marsha said. "We shall provide the brains and they shall provide the brawn." She went to the door to let the men in.

"Lexi will join us," she said. "I trust you won't mind."

"Of course not," Josh said. "Happy she's here."

"Good. Then let's strategize."

CHAPTER TWENTY-FOUR

On the next Wednesday night, two of Murray's football players visited the Loading Dock. They weren't there to commit mayhem. On the contrary, they were there to reconnoiter the place. They bought a few beers, watching some of the women in the place dance, and they went to the men's room frequently. They were checking for hidden doors, security cameras, or anything else that might be of interest. On Thursday, two other guys did the same thing. The quartet reported their findings at Shaughnessy's the following night.

"Wednesday is pretty crowded," one pair said. "We counted four bouncers, two doormen, and a male bartender helped by a female. Nothing special about the men's room: no cameras inside but a few outside, no doors other than the entry."

The Thursday scouts reported much the same, except that the crowd size inside was much smaller. They did note that one of the doormen had a couple of metal splints on his right hand and the other one seemed like he had a perpetual smirk on his face.

"It seems like a weeknight other than Wednesday is our target," Duffy said. "We want the slightest possible chance of collateral damage. Let's send a couple more guys just to check the crowd on Tuesday."

Murray agreed and added:

"It looks like the gang might be running low on troops. The guy with the broken fingers and the guy Coe took down are working. The three guys the feds took down must have hurt them."

"Maybe, but let's not take that for granted," Duffy said. "The last thing we need is for reinforcements to show up at a bad time. We need to hit them fast and hard before any guns are produced."

•••

Eight women were seated around Marsha's living room as she outlined the plan. She emphasized the need for speed also, given the possibility that the goons might be armed.

"They got to go down fast and hard," Marsha said. "We won't be carrying so we don't want to risk any shooting for our sake or that of any bystanders."

She gave them the results of Murray's scouting reports but also cautioned against underestimating their opposition.

"We know that the three guys busted by the FBI aren't talking but we don't know the exact numbers of the gang. We might know how many guys are in the club but if they have other girls stashed, someone has to be tending to them."

"About that," Denise said. "I like the idea of putting these assholes out of business for good but I don't like the idea that there might be women still being abused."

"I agree," Marsha said. "Let me worry about that aspect."

She was still speaking to the group when the hospital called.

"Lexi, come with me. Sheila, will you see to our guests? You all can stay if you like but we need to go check on some developments with Coe."

As they drove to the hospital, Marsha filled Lexi in.

"Coe had a seizure," she said.

"Oh my God! What does that mean? Is he in danger?"

"The doctors have indicated he's doing well now but we will learn more when we get to the hospital."

When they arrived at the Intensive Care Unit, Gretchen, Marsha's doctor friend, greeted them.

"I don't want you to worry," Gretchen said. "This happens occasionally in cases of traumatic brain injury. The seizure wasn't severe and didn't last very long but I thought you would like to know."

Marsha maintained her calm exterior while Lexi was shaken to the core.

"Will he recover?" she asked. "Will this be permanent? What are you doing for him?"

Gretchen moved them to a small room marked "Staff Only" and sat them both down.

"You need to relax, young lady. This happens. It is not something to worry about unless it happens repeatedly. About one in ten cases of TBI, that's traumatic brain injury, experiences seizures in the aftermath. If it happens right after the injury that's much better than if it happens later. We will just keep an eye on him and hope this was a one-time occurrence. If we need them, there are therapeutic drugs we can give him but for now, we just wait and see."

"Is Coe awake?" Marsha asked. "Can we see him?"

Gretchen opened the door and had them follow her into the ICU.

"Don't get him alarmed or excited," she said. "He's had enough of that for one day."

Marsha and Lexi went to opposite sides of Coe's bed, where he appeared to be sleeping. Lexi took his hand and his eyes opened. He smiled at Lexi and took his mother's hand.

"Nice to see you two," he said. "Something happened to me but I don't know what."

"Nothing to worry about," Marsha said. "You were probably dreaming."

Lexi bent down to kiss Coe's forehead, what little of it not covered with gauze.

"Just rest," she said. "We won't let anything bad happen to you."

Gretchen signaled to them that their time was up.

"The nurses didn't want him to have any visitors at all but when I explained what good friends of the hospital you and Coe are, they gave you five minutes," she said.

When they were in Marsha's car, Lexi asked what Gretchen meant by "friends of the hospital."

"Don't concern yourself with that, dear. Save it for Coe's recovery."

•••

Josh and Eddie decided that a full slate of reconnaissance was needed so they sent different pairs to the Loading Dock each night. They discussed staging their operation on a busy night when the staffing might have been increased and they could maximize their attack but decided to err on the side of caution and go on a Tuesday.

"It wouldn't go well for us if some innocent civilian went down because of us," Josh said, and Eddie concurred.

Then they gathered their guys to spell out the plan.

•••

"You're sure you're okay with this?" Marsha asked.

"Hell yeah, I'm sure," the Queen said. "Wouldn't miss this chance for the world."

Then she offered Marsha her fist and Marsha executed her first ever fist bump. Things were shaping up, she thought. We might actually pull this off.

CHAPTER TWENTY-FIVE

"You guys all go down to see Matty Burke at his store on Abbott," Eddie said. "He's got a few toys we might need when we visit our friends."

Two cars made their way the short distance to a tiny storefront with a sign that just said "Burky's." The place was so small, only one of the burly bouncers could make it inside at a time.

"You guys must be Murray's crew," Burky said, ushering the big man into the rear of the store. "Eddie told me you guys might need a little something extra for a play date you were having."

With that, he reached into a box and pulled out piece of wood about ten inches in length. It had a beveled handle and leather thong attached through a hole in the handle.

"This don't look like much," he told the football player, "but feel it."

Eddie's guy took it in his hand.

"They call it a tire thumper," Burky said, "but I don't think it makes much difference what, or who, you thump."

The proprietor showed Murray's guy how to loop the thong around a belt buckle and hang it inside his pants.

"Or I can give you guys these Velcro belts with a little fastener on them. Either way, you can get at them quick. You'll have no worries about metal detectors. How many guys are going to the party?"

The seven footballers left with their thumpers and Velcro belts.

Sheila was using her sweetest voice to reserve spots for Lexi's crew at the Loading Dock.

"Yes, we're having a reunion of some gals who all went to modeling school together and we were told your club might be the perfect spot for our gathering," she said. "There will be five of us. We'll see you about nine next Tuesday."

Sheila turned to her mother.

"That will keep the goons from wondering why so many beautiful women show up on an off night."

"That was a good idea," Marsha said. "The modeling thing is a nice touch. It might make the pigs at the place lick their chops.

"Things are falling in place nicely. Murray said he'll drive the limousine for Lexi and her posse. His football players slash bouncers are going to show up on their own ..."

"And do you have the *piece de resistance* all lined up?" Sheila asked

"Of course I do," Marsha said, smiling.

•••

"Do you have my package ready, Marco?" Marsha asked.

"I do," he said, "but this is a pretty big order, Marsha."

"And you will package it as we discussed?"

"Anything for you, doll. You know that."

"I do know that, Marco, but if you call me 'doll' again, I'll have your scrotum wrapped with barbed wire. Just make sure it's packaged and delivered."

She ended that call and dialed Brett Joseph at police headquarters.

"Can you get a message to your fed friends?" she asked.

"I can try," he said.

"Are you a Star Wars fan, Brett?"

"Yeah, I am."

"Well then, just remember what Yoda told Luke: 'try not, do.'"

The detective laughed and said he would 'do.'

"That's better," she said. "This is what you can tell them."

•••

Josh and Eddie sat at the bar with their beers.

"What do you think, Duffy? Is this going to work?"

"We have the best mind I know working on this," Josh said. "If Marsha says this is going to work, I believe her. It isn't exactly what I would do and I know it isn't what you would do either. But I learned a long time ago that Marsha is brilliant so I'll bite my tongue and take my lead from her.

"Besides, we'll be backing her play, so I believe it'll work."

Eddie and Josh clinked beer bottles and talked about Coe.

•••

If Ed had reservations about Marsha's plan, he wasn't alone. Lexi wasn't crazy about it either and she said so to Cat as they sat at the bar at Cole's.

"I don't know about you, my friend, but I think we should just walk in that shithole and start kicking ass," she said.

"Lexi, I know that's what you would like to do because that's what you always want to do," Cat said, "but I can see where Marsha's going with this. She's looking for the best way to do the most damage with the fewest injuries to our side. That works for me.

"Besides, I like the idea of getting all dolled up."

That got them both laughing. They clinked their wine glasses and Lexi ordered two more. Donny Joe poured and smiled.

"On Coe's tab?" he asked.

"But of course," Lexi said, grinning. "You know he'd want it this way."

"He's still doing okay?" Donnie asked.

"He needs surgery to fix his broken leg but he's as good as can be expected," Lexi said.

•••

Back on Elmwood, Dora was handing out slingers for the Loading Dock. She stopped in front of Spot Coffee when her phone rang.

"Yeah, I'm on the street," she said. "No, I haven't seen any cops. I told you the woman who used to be a cop said they were done. They wanted the soldier and his sister back and they got them. She was pretty shook up because you killed her boyfriend, though. You scared the hell out of her and her friends.

"No, I haven't found any new recruits. Don't I tell you when I do?"

When the call ended, she put the phone back in her pocket. Then she went into the coffee shop and bought a sandwich with some of Lexi's money. She decided she liked having some money in her pocket.

•••

Lexi and her crew gathered at Marsha's condo for one last meeting before the big night.

"Is everyone clear about your roles?" Marsha asked. "Please speak up now. It's important that we all know what to do at the appropriate time."

Denise spoke up.

"You mentioned gift bags that we would bring to the Loading Dock," she said. "What are they and when do we get them?"

"You will get the bags in the limo on the way to the club," Marsha said, "along with instructions as to what to do with them."

They all got up to leave and Lexi noticed the Queen wasn't among them. She approached Marsha away from the group.

"Please don't tell me Queen dropped out," Lexi said. "I really liked her."

"Don't worry, dear. Queen is still on the team and will play an important part in our mission."

Then Marsha attended to seeing her guests out.

"Be careful, ladies," she said, "Simon was drooling when you all came in."

"He better wipe and watch his mouth," Lexi said. "These women are ready to kick some ass."

"Indeed, they are," Marsha said. "Indeed, they are."

•••

Back at Shaughnessy's, Josh and Eddie were having their own final meeting.

"Try not to kill anyone," Murray said, "unless it's absolutely necessary."

The guys laughed at that.

"No shit," Murray said. "Defend yourselves all the time. I don't give a shit about the Russians but I want all of you coming back here and drinking my beer. You got that?"

Josh ended the gathering.

"You know what we need to do and you know why we need to do it. These bastards have been victimizing young girls and they damn near killed Coe. It's time we got a little payback and put these Russki pricks out of business."

CHAPTER TWENTY-SIX

Eddie drove the limousine. It was stocked with seven beautiful and dangerous women, eight counting Sheila. But Sheila would not be joining the others inside the Loading Dock. Her job was to distribute the gift bags. Each bag carried five ounces of pure heroin.

"Keep the bags with you at all times," Sheila said, "and keep them out of sight. After the fun and games, scatter them around the club in semi-conspicuous places. We want to make it look like the dope was hidden but we don't want the searchers to miss it.

"We can handle these despicable bastards our own way but we want to put them permanently out of business.

"Everyone have their pot stickers?"

The women nodded and Sheila left the vehicle.

"This is going to be a hoot," Denise said. "I'm getting goose bumps just thinking about it."

Lexi wanted them calm, at least in the beginning.

"I think we are all anxious to do some damage," she said, "but we've got to play it cool until the shit hits the fan. Let's not blow our cover until we have to."

Murray started the car and headed to Exchange Street. Ten minutes later, two SUVs carrying four football players each headed to the same destination. Unknown to either group, another limo was on its way to the same destination. That car pulled up to the door and two women made their way inside but not before the doormen on duty eyed them up and down. One of them had metal splints on his fingers. He watched her walk and mumbled "kraseevaia zhenshchina" (beautiful woman). And beautiful she was, with striking black hair perfectly framing her face and a tight black knit dress that clung to her curves and ended just below the knee. Her companion was beautiful in her own right, but she was just second best when standing beside her friend. The two women made their way to the bar, sat, and surveyed the club. The bartender joined them and asked what they wanted.

"A little action would be nice," the black-haired beauty said. "This place is dead."

"Things pick up in about an hour," the bartender said. "It's still early."

"What do you think?" the woman asked her friend. "Should we get out of here?"

"We're here," her friend said. "We might as well have a drink."

She spoke to the bartender.

"Bring us two cosmos," she said, placing a hundred-dollar bill on the bar.

The bartender started pouring and mixing and placed the cocktails in front of the ladies and took the bill from the bar.

The raven-haired woman took a sip and made a face.

"Are you out of lime juice or are you too dumb to put it in the drink?"

The bartender stared at the woman coldly but thought better of saying anything. He rung up the charge and put seventy dollars back on the bar.

"For fifteen dollars a pop, you might think you'd get a drink made by a pro," the friend said. The two women smiled at each other and high-fived. The bartender was not pleased and walked down the bar.

"I think it's time," the black-haired woman said and her friend nodded. Then she touched a pin on her dress and a small camera hidden in a brooch she wore turned on. Then she slid her drink away from her.

"Bartender, this is undrinkable," she said. "Bring me a Manhattan."

The bartender glared at her for a minute, then started mixing her drink.

Her friend asked the bartender where the ladies' room was, and he gestured to the right.

"It's just down that hall," he said. "It'll have a sign that says 'ladies,' but don't let that stop you."

"Oh my," the friend said, "he's just as bad at making jokes as he is making drinks."

Both of the women laughed. The bartender didn't. The friend started down the hallway but turned and went back to the bar in time to see the bartender put a cherry in the drink before adding a squirt of something else. The camera caught the action. She sat back down and whispered to her friend.

"I think he dosed you."

The black-haired woman nodded. Her friend took her purse from the bar and put it in her lap. The bartender returned with the drink and took more cash off the bar. While his back was turned, the friend opened her purse while the other woman poured much of the drink into the bag.

She spoke softly to her friend.

"Glad we lined this with plastic. I like this purse."

"Looks like the other gals have shown up," the black-haired woman said, looking toward the door.

Six women came in laughing and talking.

"Looks like our friends clean up nicely," she said. "Who would have thought cops could look that hot?"

A couple of the women looked their way, but it was Lexi who was staring. The woman with the purse saw Lexi's attention and mouthed a silent 'no' to her so Lexi looked away and started talking with the other women. They got seated at a round table and ordered drinks. Before their drinks arrived, eight burly guys came in and sat at the bar. Only three other patrons were in the place. With the bartender's attention diverted to the newcomers, the black-haired lady dumped the rest of her drink into her friend's purse.

"Tell me you got this piece of shit dosing my drink," she said. Her friend tapped her brooch and smiled.

"I got him."

"Come on," she said. "Let's dance. I need to do something for another half hour or so to sell this."

The two women headed to the dance floor with their bodies gyrating under the strobe lights. They drew quite an audience as they shimmied and twerked and moved to the music. Even the doormen left their posts to watch the display of raw sexiness on the floor.

Lexi watched from her table and knew the other women were watching too.

"Holy shit," Lexi said. "I don't know who that is but she's making me horny."

That drew a punch on the arm from Cat.

"Focus, dear one, and remember your dear one is still in the hospital."

They laughed and clinked glasses. Then Lexi rose and made it out to the middle of the dance floor. She got the attention of the raven-haired woman and beckoned her out to join her. The woman left her seat at the bar and joined Lexi. Their little pas-de-deux started slowly but soon evolved into a dance-off to determine the sexiest dancer. The pair bumped and gyrated and twirled and humped and sweated. The guys at the bar started hooting and hollering. The girls at the table started clapping in time with the music. The two women ground it out for another minute or two before the women from Lexi's table got up and joined in. Lexi was about to head for the table when her partner pulled her close and whispered.

"It's Queen," she said before kissing her on the mouth. "Don't blow my cover."

The black-haired beauty returned to the bar, leaving Lexi stunned and out of breath. She made her way back to the table while the other women danced up a storm. Lexi then realized there were parts of the plan that she wasn't privy to. She stared at Queen and wondered what she was up to. She didn't have a lot of time to wonder. Denise made her way back to the table and motioned toward the door.

"Some civilians are making their way in," she said. "We better get started or we might have some collateral damage."

"Give it a few minutes," Lexi said, still trying to wrap her head around the new development.

•••

Brett Joseph was working his contacts at the federal building.

"This is Detective Joseph with Buffalo PD. Is Jackson Barrett available?"

A minute later, Barrett was on the phone.

"What have you got for me this time, Brett?" he asked. "Please don't tell me about some guys selling meth on the west side."

"Okay, I'll save that one for later. Tonight, I have something you might really be able to sink your teeth into."

"I'll be the judge of that. Give me some details."

Joseph explained the tip he got about heroin making its way to the Loading Dock before being sold to middlemen who would take it to various parts of western New York for distribution.

"So, how much dope are we talking about?" Barrett asked.

"My guy says thirty to forty kilos."

"Why aren't your guys handling it?"

"We have some plumbing issues we're still trying to correct."

"Plumbing like leaks?"

"You got it," Joseph said. Then he gave the DEA agent a time that he thought would allow the Lexi team enough time to spread the wealth. As soon as their call ended, Barrett started making calls of his own.

•••

The Queen's partner turned slightly toward the end of the bar just as one of Murray's guys came to the bar. She started filming and recording again.

The football player summoned the bartender.

"What do you need, pal?"

"I want a beer, but I need some of that stuff you guys use to dose the chicks around here."

The bartender started to walk away and spoke over his shoulder.

"I don't know what you are talking about."

Murray's guy put a fifty-dollar bill on the bar.

"This about cover it?" he asked.

The bartender walked back to him slowly.

"That covers one pill, dude, but that's all you'll need. This is potent shit." Then he went to a cooler, pulled out a Budweiser, placed it on the bar along with a little plastic bag containing a pill. He slid the fifty off the bar and slipped it in his pocket. He never saw the tiny marking on the corner of the bill. It wouldn't have mattered much if he had because the transaction was now on film.

Behind the camera girl, the Queen was starting to feign dizziness. She stood and tried to shake off the effects of the drug she faked taking. She sat back down and put her head on the bar.

"Sweetie, I'm feeling a little off," she said to her friend in a loud voice. "I'm going to the ladies' room for a minute or two."

Then she wobbled her way toward the door. As she did, the bartender pressed a button under the bar. The camera girl did the same with a button on the strap of her purse.

The Queen entered the ladies' room and went to a stall to sit down and act a little out of it. It didn't take long before a hidden door in an adjacent stall opened and a bulky man moved quickly into the Queen's stall and held a towel over her face to stifle any screams. She put up a feeble fight and tried yelling out, but the towel absorbed most of the noise. The guy roughly pulled her to her feet and into the stall with the hidden door. In less than a minute, she was out of the club and in a dark room whose only light came from the other side of the room. The Queen acted out her role, dragging her feet and mumbling some weak protests. She quickly felt the cool outside air on her face and knew their ploy was working. Her only concern now was that the tracking device was activated and either Marsha or Josh was ready. She needn't have worried. When the camera girl touched her button, Both Marsha and Josh got signals. Both were waiting outside, Marsha on Exchange Street and Josh near the tracks behind the Loading

Dock, and ready to follow wherever the thug was taking the Queen. Marsha saw the guy half-dragging the Queen to a panel truck a hundred or so yards from the club.

The Queen is not only a beauty, Marsha thought, but she's a hell of an actress. She hit a button on her phone and Josh answered.

The guy roughly tossed her into the truck. As he did, the Queen's dress slid over her thighs. The thug shoved his hand up her dress and rubbed her through her panties. While he was playing, the driver of the truck came back to the door. He greedily looked up her dress before squeezing her tits.

"Etot prineset mnogo deneg." (This one will bring a lot of money.)

The Queen had all she could do to stop from beating the shit out of the pair. I'm going to really enjoy kicking your asses, she thought to herself.

The two guys finished fondling their new catch, closed the door, and headed west on Exchange toward downtown.

"White panel truck, heading toward downtown," she said.

"Got it. I'll pull around."

There was no need for either Marsha or Josh to drive too close as the Queen's locator button was working just fine.

•••

Back at the Loading Dock, things were beginning to percolate.

Queen's companion was looking for her friend and went to the ladies' room where she found no trace of her. She went back to the bar and screamed at the bartender.

"What the fuck happened to my friend?"

The bartender hardly changed his expression.

"What are you talking about? You didn't come in here with a friend. You were alone."

"Look, asshole, you better start talking or some shit is going to go down you won't like."

"Who the fuck are you calling an 'asshole,' bitch? Time for you to leave."

With that, he nodded to one of the doormen who approached the woman quickly. Just as quick, though, Lexi left her table and came to the bar.

"What are you trying to pull here?" Lexi asked. "This woman had a friend with her, and I danced with her. What's going on?"

The other women at Lexi's table knew the game was on and made their way to the bar. Denise pointed to the bouncer.

"You know goddamned right well she had a friend," she said. "This Neanderthal was drooling all over himself watching her dance. Someone better start coming up with some answers pretty damned quick."

The bouncer put his hand on Denise's shoulder, and she erupted. Her left hand smashed into the guy's throat with lightning speed and high impact. His eyes bulged and he started gasping for breath when her knee connected with his balls. He didn't know which to grab as the pain swept over him. The second bouncer ran in to help but Ginna shot out her right leg and caught him on the kneecap, bending his leg a way it wasn't made to bend. He crumpled to the floor just in time to catch a straight right hand to the nose from Cat. The footballers from Murray's now enthusiastically joined the fray. The bartender hit another button under the bar and three more goons came in from the ladies' room door. Murray's guys slipped the tire thumpers from their belts and started wailing. One of the thugs went down immediately after a blow to the temple. Another one produced a blackjack and started swinging at the boys. Lindsay put an end to that threat with a stun gun to the goon's neck. He went down convulsing and was effectively out of the fight. The third goon pulled a gun from his waistband but never got to use it. A chopping motion from a thumper knocked the gun from his hand and an elbow turned his nose into bloody pulp. He went to his knees and Lexi approached from the side to give the thug a dose of his own medicine; not exactly his own medicine but a twenty-milligram dose of Versed put him out cold. Cat dosed another guy and Maria stuck the third guy. The bartender made a feeble attempt to fight back but quickly thought better of the idea. He placed his hands, palms down, on the bar, taking himself out of the fight. The Queen's friend smiled at him and whispered something to him. He leaned over toward her to hear what she said but that was a mistake. She shot the hell of her right hand out, catching him under the nose and knocking him to the floor.

"No one calls me a bitch," she said. "Dose this motherfucker before I kill him."

She looked over the bar at him cowering on the floor, spitting up blood. "I still might, you little weasel, if anything happens to my friend."

Murray's guys were hustling the civilians out of the club while Lexi and friends were making the rounds of the place stashing five kilo bags of heroin in beer coolers, under the bar, and anywhere else that might look like a suitable hiding place. The contraband stashed, the goons now asleep, and everything buttoned down, Lexi's posse and the footballers were out the door.

•••

As the truck bounced along city streets, the Queen was formulating her plan. The first thing she needed to do was sell her deep sleep. The Ambien would have been in full effect now so she had to convince the kidnappers she was out of it. She hoped she was being taken to somewhere the other women were being held. It was paramount to the entire operation to rescue everyone being held by the Russians. If she was being isolated, her plan would be simple. She would kill or disable whomever she encountered. If the other women were in play, she'd have to be more nuanced, at least at the outset. Putting the captives in harm's way was not an option. She did, of course, have her tracker on and her movements should be followed by whomever Marsha had tailing her. But the Queen knew better that to assume a strategy would work as planned. She steeled herself to face a situation where she was alone. She felt the truck slowing. She felt the distance they'd traveled wasn't very far. That meant the others were being held close to the Loading Dock or that something else was afoot. It was something else.

The truck stopped and the Queen heard the passenger door open. The driver and his sidekick sounded like they were arguing in Russian.

"Ya khochu trakhnut' yeye!" the driver said. (I want to fuck her.)

"Don't damage the goods," the other guy said.

It was then Queen figured out what the driver was saying. She wasn't ready for this. If the driver did, indeed, want to fuck her, what would she do? She could easily disable the guy and his partner also but what did that mean for the other women? If the two assholes were out of commission, how would she ever find the others? She was not a virgin but the thought of the scummy Russian violating her was enough to make her vomit. She decided she had to take it if they were going to complete the mission. The side door opened and the driver stuck his hand up Queen's dress. His rough hand moved aside her panties and he jammed his finger inside her.

"Da, eto khorosho," he said (Yeah, this is good.)

Queen had all she could do to remain still while he continued his assault. She thought she heard the sound of his zipper and steeled herself for the worst. But the partner's phone rang.

"Armen, stop! There is trouble and we need to go!"

"What trouble?" the driver said. "This won't take long."

"The politsiya (police) have raided the club and Volkov says we must return at once."

The driver mumbled something in Russian and zipped his pants before climbing into the truck. He sped down Michigan Avenue, away from downtown, and turned onto Ohio Street. A mile later, he pulled into the parking lot of an abandoned warehouse next to a junkyard. Not far behind, Marsha and Josh pulled over to see which door the Russians used.

"Keeping the women next to a working junkyard means they wouldn't be heard even if they were in any shape to cry out," Josh said.

"What's our next play?" Marsha asked.

"Murman and Lexi's posse just pulled in behind us," Josh said. "The football players will be right behind them. We've got numbers, so I say we go in hot. The raid probably went down already so these guys will be trying to get away as clean as they can."

Marsha buzzed Murray on her phone and told them the plan. He said he'd drop off his team and go around to the back to make sure no one escaped that way.

Josh looked at his ex-wife.

"You ready if things get heavy?"

"You bet," she said, patting her thigh.

Queen was yanked out of the truck, but her legs weren't working so well so the driver threw her over his shoulder. Her dress was all the way over her ass, and she was thankful the charade would be ending soon. The driver's partner banged on the steel door, and it opened. They entered and Queen opened one eye to survey the place. Her cavalry wouldn't arrive until they were sure the other women were here. She was in a large empty space with no one else in sight except her captors and three other men who were very interested in the sight of Queen's panty clad ass. One of the guys ran his hand over her butt and growled.

"Etot moy." (This one is mine.)

Queen figured him for the alpha and couldn't wait to take his ass down. He barked some orders in Russian and a couple of guys headed for a doorway near the back of the building. The driver carried Queen to another doorway and kicked it open, revealing a single bed with an un-sheeted mattress. He threw her on the bed and left the room. It didn't take long for the alpha to enter. Queen's eyes were open just wide enough see him lick his lips and unzip with pants. He leaned forward to grab her and ripped her panties off. His eyes were greedy with lust, and he moved to enter her but got a big surprise when he did. In a single rapid movement, Queen grabbed his scrotum with one hand and jammed her knuckles into his throat. His eyes bulged and he gasped for breath as she hit him hard on the ear. The pain contorted his face before Queen's palm smacked into his nose. She rolled off the bed and threw him on to it. She punched hard into his balls. She then grabbed his broken nose and twisted.

"Where are the other girls?" she asked. He didn't answer fast enough, so she kneed him in the nuts. "Where?"

He pointed to the left, where he had sent the other two goons.

"In here? In this building?"

He nodded a yes before she produced a syringe from her bra strap and gave him a good night dose of Versed. She kept her hand on his nose until he started to blink and finally passed out. She searched him for keys and a possible gun and found only a large ring of keys. She straightened her dress and walked back into the big room. Two thugs were standing around.

"Okay, who's next?" she said, smiling. She pulled the bodice of her dress down to reveal her lacy bra. The boys thought it a "come on" for them but she pressed a small button on the strap and the door banged open as Josh, Marsha, and company charged in. As they did, Queen was already moving toward the door that kept the other women captive. The driver came out that door and this time, Queen licked her lips. He threw a right-hand punch at her that she easily dodged. She pulled his arm straight, then jammed her elbow behind his, breaking his arm. He swung his left arm in a feeble motion that she sidestepped. She jammed her left leg on to the outside of his left knee. He crumpled to his knees and stayed there until Denise kneed him in the face. She and Queen high-fived. Lexi led the rest of her crew toward the door Queen pointed out. Josh was about to follow but Marsha held him back.

"The strong women have awakened," she said. "Let them do the saving."

Josh nodded his assent as the women made their way into the room holding the captives. One of the Russians was still in the room trying to round them up. Apparently, the gang was planning on moving the women to another location. That wasn't happening now. Lexi moved on him, balancing on the balls of her feet. He grinned at the prospect of beating at least one woman's ass. He waded in close and Lexi bitch-slapped him with a lightning-fast left hand. The smile left his face and he bull-rushed her. She side stepped him and smashed an elbow into his ear. The thug staggered a little and turned to make another charge. He never got the chance. Cat Redmond came from the back and jabbed the stun gun against his neck. Lexi looked pissed off.

"We don't have time for your martial arts display," Cat said. "Let's just say you kicked his ass and be done with it."

They laughed while Lindsay stuck the needle with the Versed into his arm. He squirmed a little and she hastened his nap with a driving punch to his jaw. The rest of the team went about collecting the captives and getting them out to the limousine. There were nine, all dressed in shabby bathrobes and housedresses. Some of them had cigarette burn marks on their arms. A few were bare-footed. They all looked dazed. Once situated in the big car, Lexi's team gave them water to help them hydrate. Eddie Murray climbed in behind the wheel.

"The county hospital?" he asked.

"Yes," Marsha said. "Sheila should already be there. She was making the arrangements to have the women checked out."

Murray was about to drive off when he heard Josh yell.

"Marsha, look out!"

The lothario who thought the Queen was going to be his dessert this night must have shaken off the effects of the Versed. He was stumbling toward the limo, waving an axe.

"I got him," Marsha said calmly. She reached under her dress and pulled a .9mm pistol from her garter. The asshole was about ten feet away when Marsha fired two rounds, both striking him in the chest. He went down like a bag of rocks.

"Holy shit!" Lexi yelled.

"No worries, darling," Marsha said. "They were rubber bullets; a far better fate than he deserved."

Queen came over to Marsha's side.

"Any more bullets in there?" she asked.

"Seven more," Marsha said.

"May I?" Queen asked.

"Be my guest," Marsha said.

Queen took the pistol and walked over to the prone gangster. He was fading from consciousness rapidly, so Queen pulled up her dress revealing her splendid nakedness.

"Hey Romeo, you still want this?"

The goon's eyes widened. Then she shot him in the balls with a rubber bullet.

EPILOGUE

Coe's eyes widened when his mother reached into her purse and produced his electric toothbrush. He looked like a kid opening a Christmas present.

"Holy shit, Marsha," he said. "My prayers have been answered."

Lexi was mystified.

"What? You haven't been brushing your teeth?"

"Not with this beauty," he said. "Using the giveaway toothbrushes here has been a pain. They scratch my gums and still leave my teeth feeling like they have mittens on them."

He stroked the electric model gently before putting it on his hospital nightstand. Then, he made a face at Lexi.

"So you didn't have the decency to wait for me to crash the Loading Dock," he said. "I really appreciate that. Now I'll never have a chance to get some payback for what those bastards did to me. Thanks for that."

Lexi laughed.

"We got all the payback you would ever need and then some," she said. "The ladies were out-damned-standing."

Coe had heard an abridged version of the assault on the Loading Dock from his father but he assumed that he was hearing an exaggerated version of the events, but hearing a similar story from his sister Sheila, he realized he'd missed quite a show. He made Lexi come to the hospital to get a third version of the story just to make sure of the salient details. Both the Lexi and Sheila versions highlighted the courage and prowess of the woman they knew as Queen.

"Where the hell did she come from?" Coe asked. "If she was from around here, we would have all known about her before now."

Marsha answered his question.

"Her parents emigrated from Israel to Canada, but Agatha, who we know as Queen, stayed behind to spend time in the army. She was in their special forces and later in Mossad, the Israeli intelligence service. She ended her service as part of Metsada, a special branch of Mossad."

"Damn, she was a hell of a find for us," Coe said. "But how did you pick her for the dirty work?"

"I didn't pick her," Marsha said. "She picked herself. If you recall, she had a run in with one of the bouncers at the Loading Dock and broke a couple of his fingers, so I wanted to disqualify her as she would be known to the thugs at the club.

"But she took me aside and told me of her background. I knew then she would be perfect for the job of finding the other captives. All we needed to do was cover up those blonde locks of hers and we'd be ready."

Lexi pouted a bit and wanted to change the subject.

"How's the leg coming?" she asked.

"The doc said he wanted me getting mobile with a walker soon," Coe said. "If I take the rehab seriously, he told me I should be good in a couple months."

"And we know how seriously you take everything," Marsha said.

Sheila came into the room, carrying an arrangement of roses. She put them on the nightstand and gave him a kiss on the forehead.

"This bit of news should help in your recovery," she said. "I spoke with Brett Joseph at police headquarters, and he indicated that his DEA guy Jackson Barrett and his crew had eleven men in custody on drug charges. The other feds have them on interstate movement of stolen property, and various other charges. Some of them were wanted by Interpol, so jurisdictional issues are being hashed out. The upshot is we won't see these goons around anymore."

That brought a smile to Coe's face.

"We still have yet to identify the leak from either the police or the SLA," Lexi said, "but we can work on that when you are back on your feet."

"One other thing," Sheila said. "A fire destroyed the Loading Dock and several other structures on Exchange Street last night."

Coe looked at Lexi and they both mouthed "Murman" at the same time. Marsha indicated the visit was over and that her son needed rest. The group was getting ready to leave when a stricken look came over Coe's face. He saw Dora, the waif who put all this machinery in motion, standing in the door. Coe pointed to Dora but they others laughed.

"I used some of my influence to get the girl you call Dora a job," Marsha said. "Her real name is Bella, though, and you should be nice to her. She's in training to become a nurse's aide and she is working on this floor."

Bella entered the room with an armful of supplies.

"Hello, Mr. Duffy, I'm here to give you your sponge bath," Bella said.

"Oh hell no," Coe said. "Hell no!"

-end-

ACKNOWLEDGEMENTS

No book would ever see the light of day without the services of a fine editor and Ellie Rummell ably filled that role for me. I also owe my wife, Shirley, special thanks for her keen eye in pointing out places to tighten my plot and make the book more readable.

Amy Fleischauer, the Director of Survivor Support Services at the International Institute provided valuable information about the extent and depth of the problem of human trafficking in Western New York.

Detective Dave Mann of the Buffalo Police Department provided specific insights into the scope and details of the crisis as it relates to Buffalo and his input gave the plot its direction.

Matty Burke is one of the legendary yet behind the scenes personalities in South Buffalo and owner of Burky's.

Denise Crawford is a retired Buffalo police officer and Lindsay Zgoda is currently still on the force. Their inclusion is a tribute to all those women who have served and still serve in law enforcement and as first responders throughout Western New York.

Karen Connors Erickson and her family completed their 78th year of operation at Connors Hot Dog stand, a true landmark on our lakeshore.

Joe Jerge and Tim Eberle are proprietors at the Mulberry restaurant where Italian food at its finest is served. Bea Montione at the Bijou is one of our city's finest restauranteurs, and Cole's and Dave Shatzel Sr. are long-standing Buffalo legends.

About the Author

This is Steve Banko's second book featuring Coe and Lexi and his third novel, all written since his 70th birthday. He is a three-time recipient of the Gold Medal from the National VA Creative Arts Festival and has spoken to audiences around the country on issues of war and peace.

He served sixteen months in Vietnam combat, earning the Silver Star for valor in combat and four Bronze Stars for Valor. He also received four Purple Hearts for wounds he sustained.

If you enjoyed this book, you might like the first one, "Dark Shadows at Central Terminal."

Made in the USA
Columbia, SC
14 February 2023

12121132R00126